"You got Jamie the doll, right?" Liz asked her husband.

Howard looked at her in confusion. "The doll?"

Liz fluffed up her pillow. "The Turbo Man doll," she said around a yawn. "I asked you to pick one up. Two weeks ago."

"Oh." Howard made a sour face. "*That* doll."

Liz stared at her husband with dismay. "Oh, Howard! I can't believe you forgot!"

"What?" Howard batted his eyes in confusion. "No. I didn't forget. I got it." He closed his eyes and snuggled down into the pillow. "The Turbo Man doll. With the thing that shoots . . . and the rockem-sockem jet pack." A yawn halted him for a second. "And the realistic voice box that says, 'It's Turbo Time.' Of course, I got the doll."

"Good," said Liz, putting out the light. "Because at this point, they'd probably be impossible to find."

In the dark, Howard's eyes snapped open.

Jingle All The Way

A Novelization by David Cody Weiss
and Bobbi JG Weiss
Based on the Screenplay by RANDY KORNFIELD

Published by POCKET BOOKS
New York London Toronto Sydney Tokyo Singapore

A MINSTREL PAPERBACK *Original*

A Minstrel Book published by
POCKET BOOKS, a division of Simon & Schuster Inc.
1230 Avenue of the Americas, New York, NY 10020

ISBN: 0-671-00426-3

First Minstrel Books printing December 1996

10 9 8 7 6 5 4 3 2 1

Photos courtesy of Twentieth Century Fox, Inc.
Photos by Murray Close

Printed in the U.S.A.

Jingle All The Way

1

In the television studio of a great metropolitan center, all the monitors interrupted regular programming with a brightly colored Special Bulletin announcement card. An anchorman sped toward his news desk, weaving effortlessly through the seeming chaos of a crew jumping on a breaking story. Around the desk, cameramen wheeled into position, techs scurried to adjust lights and microphones, and a stage manager counted backward.

"Five . . . four . . . three . . . two . . ." Instead of saying "one," the stage director silently pointed his index finger directly at the news anchorman, a handsome man with the build of a football player. The anchorman, Ed McGuire, began to speak to the camera.

"The President, First Lady, and their son, Billy, have been kidnapped by the evil mutant, Dementor!" Ed fixed a steely eye on the camera lens, peering into the heart of America. "All across the country, helpless citizens are asking *one* question . . ." The camera zoomed in, the studio monitors filling with Ed's face. *"Turbo Man, where are you?"*

The news-show producer clapped the cameraman on the back, yelling, "And—cut!" He turned toward the news desk. "Good job, Ed." But Ed was gone, his empty chair spinning behind the desk. "Ed . . . *Ed?"*

Ed ran down the hall toward a storage room near the studio, loosening his tie and shucking off his jacket on the way. A moment later, a flash of jet-propelled red and gold zoomed out of the storage-room window and up into the sky. America's question had been answered: Turbo Man was on the way!

The alien spacecraft nestled in a corner of a rocky box canyon that was colored the dusty gray of a moonscape. From beneath the spacecraft, a trio of battle-suited thugs wearing helmets that looked like saltshakers hustled the First Family down a ramp to the ground. The prisoners—the President, the First Lady, and their son, nine-year-old Billy—their hands tied securely behind their backs, were marched from the ship and across the floor of the canyon to the base of an enormous megacannon.

The President, a middle-aged man whose plump face

bore the manner of someone who was more used to giving orders than taking them, grumbled under his breath each time his guards shoved him to direct his movement. His wife, with her impeccable wardrobe, her stylishly coiffed hair, and her much-tucked face, tried to pretend that this was all just a distasteful dream. Only young Billy faced his captors with open defiance, thrusting out his chin and looking around for their captor, the evil Dementor.

A hum of power split the silence, and the grinding of gears rattled the ground as the barrel of the great weapon suddenly lifted slowly, pointing up into the blackness of space. A large display screen in the control bay at the base of the weapon lit up, creating a pool of light in the shadow of the gray cliffs into which a sinister figure strode.

"So, Mr. President," called Dementor, his green cape swirling as he walked, the bright light winking off his blue-and-green battle armor. "Would you care to take a look?" He gestured toward the display with one steel gauntlet.

The display screen showed a view of a blue-and-white marble against a black background, quartered by cross-hairs centered on North America. The President's eyes widened in shock. "Why . . . that's the Earth!" He gasped.

Dementor turned to the President and mimed shock. "Well, I guess public opinion must be wrong," he purred. "You're not a *complete* moron." The villain quaked with laughter. He gave a hand signal, and his three henchmen, the Demon Team, hustled the prisoners back against the canyon wall. There they watched in horror as Dementor punched buttons and flipped switches to arm the megacannon. As he worked, Dementor called over his shoulder, "In a few minutes my Nega-Gun will be fully activated, and when fired at your pathetic planet, will completely eliminate its so-called gravity! And then taxes won't be the only things that keep rising, *hee hee hee!*"

The First Lady wept, trying to block out Dementor's insane cackle. Next to her, the President tried to bargain with the evil mutant. "Look, maybe we can cut a deal here. You want a Cabinet post? How about . . ." He thought hard. "Uh, Secretary of Evil?"

"Save your breath, Mr. President," Dementor sneered. "You're going to need it."

Suddenly one of the canyon walls erupted in a shower of rocks and dust. "Look!" shouted Billy. "It's Turbo Man and Booster!"

Out of the billowing cloud of debris, a muscular male figure descended to the ground on a stem of flame that blasted from a jetpack on his back. Gleaming golden boots settled onto lunar soil as the hero landed, hands on hips in classic superhero style. A second behind and a tad off-center, Turbo Man's faithful sidekick, Booster, also landed. The pink saber-toothed tiger reared back on his hind legs and imitated Turbo Man's stance.

"Drop your weapons and release the President and

his family, you twisted madman!" Turbo Man always got straight to the point.

"Spare me the heroic posturing, you pathetic do-gooder," Dementor snarled. He made a hand signal to the Demon Team. "Kill them both!"

Booster cowered to the ground, just as deadly ray-beams converged right where his head would have been if he had not ducked. Turbo Man easily dodged the fire aimed at him, diving forward and continuing in a roll. He snapped out of the roll, firing dozens of shiny Turbo-Disks at the Demon Team. Each and every one hit its mark, slicing armor, short-circuiting battle electronics, and causing killer headaches when they hit the Demons' helmets.

Dementor's thugs fell from their perches or fled in fear, but Dementor doggedly continued his Nega-Gun adjustments. Turbo Man and Booster raced toward the Nega-Gun but were attacked by reinforcement Demon Team fighters, who dropped onto them from the canyon walls.

Dementor cackled madly as he punched one last button on the console. The control pod suddenly sparkled with the lights of alien electronics powering up. A mighty vibration almost beyond hearing gathered itself around the Nega-Gun. The video display shifted to a digital counter set at thirty. A computer voice announced, "ACTIVATION IN THIRTY SECONDS."

Turbo Man punched the closest Demon. The hapless thug flew backward, toppling four more of his mates.

Across the way, the threat of Booster's foot-long fangs kept the rest of the Demons pinned into a pocket of the stony wall.

Running short of expendable hirelings, Dementor took matters into his own hands. He sped over to the imprisoned First Family and snatched the President's son.

"Help, Turbo Man! Help!" cried Billy.

Turbo Man threw a Demon twenty feet to knock out another Demon who had been trying to sneak up behind Booster. His head snapped toward the boy. "I'm coming, Billy!" he shouted.

As Turbo Man ran toward Dementor, the evil mutant pinned Billy to his chest with his right arm. Then Dementor raised his left arm and sighted along the top of its oversize steel fist. "Ta ta, Turbo!" he cackled.

Boom! The fist launched itself from Dementor's arm and rocketed straight toward Turbo Man. It caught the hero square on the chin, tumbling him backward into the gray dust, where he lay unmoving.

Turbo Man was down.

Dementor laughed triumphantly, dropped the box and disappeared in a billowing cloud of smoke.

Billy ran over to Turbo Man's body. "Turbo Man!" he pleaded. The fallen hero shuddered, then struggled to lift his head.

The computer voice announced, "FIVE SECONDS TO IGNITION."

The President shouted, "Hurry, Turbo Man, hurry!"

Turbo Man staggered halfway to his feet, pulling his collapsible Turbo-Rang from its boot sheath. The golden arc snapped open and Turbo Man flung it with all his might at the Nega-Gun controls.

The razor-edged weapon plowed into the electronic brain of the Nega-Gun controls, slicing wires and shattering circuit boards. Sparks flew and the console burst into flame.

The computer voice announced, "NEGA-GUN—DEACTIvateddd . . ." It stuttered to a halt. The hum of power that had been gathering around the weapon died away, leaving the gray canyon in silence.

For a moment, anyway. Turbo Man whirled around at the sound of the First Lady screaming. She pointed toward the top of the canyon where Turbo Man caught sight of Dementor standing on the highest edge, holding a struggling Billy. The canyon floor lay hundreds of feet beneath the boy's kicking sneakers.

Though Dementor's eyes blazed with furious madness, his voice was tight and calm. "You destroyed my antigravity gun. What a shame." He hung Billy a little farther over the edge. "Just when Billy's about to perform a little gravity experiment of his *own* . . ." And Dementor released his grip.

Turbo Man fired up his jet pack and launched himself into the air on a column of fire. Lightning calculations flashed through his brain, and with a precise twist, he arced under Billy and caught the plummeting boy in his arms.

His momentum carried them both high up over the canyon wall. From above, they could see Dementor rant in fury. "You haven't seen the last of me, Turbo Man! I'll have my revenge!" He pressed a button on his helmet, and billows of dense smoke poured out and wrapped themselves around the supervillain. Within seconds, the smoke cloud blotted out everything. . . .

The smoke was abruptly replaced by the Turbo Man show logo, and an announcer boomed: "We'll return to *Turbo Man* after these important announcements."

"Jamie?" a sweet feminine voice called. "Why don't you run upstairs and get changed? It's almost time to leave."

Eight-year-old Jamie Langston didn't leave his place in front of the television set. "But Dad's not home yet," he shouted back to his mother.

Liz Langston glanced at the clock on the wall. She tried the cheerful approach. "He's just running a little late, honey. He's probably going to meet us there straight from work. Now, go on. . . ."

Jamie looked back at the TV as the commercials ended. "That's what he always says." A look of disappointment filled his face. "He promised we'd go together."

On the screen, Turbo Man, with Billy safe in his arms, landed in front of the President and First Lady, who had just been untied by Booster. "Thanks, Turbo Man!"

Billy said with a smile as his parents hugged him. "You always show up right on time!"

Turbo Man snapped a crisp salute to Billy and replied with his motto: "You can always count on me!"

Jamie clicked off the TV as the credits started to roll and trudged toward the stairs. He frowned at his mother. "He's probably gonna miss me get my belt. He misses everything."

"Well, he's not going to miss this," Liz said, forcing optimism into her voice.

Jamie halted halfway up the stairs. "Did he call?"

His mother's cheeriness faltered. "No . . ." she admitted. "But I'm sure he's moving as fast as he possibly can. . . ."

Jamie made a wry face and continued up the stairs.

2

As loud as the Christmas party in the warehouse was, Howard Langston barely noticed it. In his office high above the work floor, he hunched over his desk, immersed in the battle called Work.

The office held the feel of a command post. Three fax machines, two computers, and three printers fed constant updates from the sales front into the little room. Massive swatch books of fabric samples fought with telephone directories and business ledgers for space across the desk and floor. The walls were occupied by photographed achievements: Howard winning wrestling trophies, Howard getting married, Howard and Liz holding newborn Jamie, Howard shaking the hands of smiling customers. And in the middle of one wall, set off from all the other photos by a ring of empty space, was a shot of Howard, Liz, and a seven-year-old Jamie aboard a sailboat in turquoise water.

Howard was a big, burly man. With his aggressive size and the symbols of his business and home life surrounding him, there wasn't much space left in the small office.

The door opened, letting in the sound of the party full blast. Howard didn't look up until his secretary shouted over the racket, "I know you didn't want to be interrupted, but you've got four calls holding!" She shot a hopeful smile at her boss. "Why don't I just tell everyone to call back after the holiday?"

Howard lifted his head. "No," he said. "It's okay, Margaret. Put them through."

Margaret pursed her lips. "But Jamie's karate class starts in twenty minutes."

"I'm gonna make it," Howard said reassuringly.

Margaret raised her eyebrows.

"I'm gonna make it!" declared Howard.

Margaret sighed. "Royal Hotels on one. Vista Resorts on two. SleepWell Bedding on three." She turned to leave. "Oh, and your wife's on four."

The door closed and the party noise retreated. Howard punched the first glowing button on his phone. "Mr. Jacobs! What can I do for you?" He shifted the phone and started writing on a pad. "Two hundred king-size by next Friday? No problem. But only for you, Mr. Jacobs. You're my number one customer!"

Howard punched the second glowing button, moving to the next call. "Andrea? Hi. . . . You think the fabric's too dark? Then I'll re-cover them. No extra charge. What else do you expect? You're my number one customer!"

Punch. Third glowing button out. "Bob . . . what's up? The box springs will be done next week. I'll ship them to you overnight. Don't forget, you're my number one customer!"

Punch. The last light extinguished. "Liz? Hi, honey." Howard twirled his pen. "I know . . . Jamie's class. Twenty minutes. I'll see you there. Remember, you're my number one customer!" Howard's jaw fell. "I mean . . . sorry. I didn't mean that." The phone was silent. "Liz? Liz?"

Howard knew he'd blundered. *Hey, I'm busy,* he thought. And that reminded him that he had to address his employees before he left. He climbed down the stairs from his office and shouldered his way through the party, exchanging greetings and handshakes along the way. He finally stopped and, raising his voice, addressed the crowd.

"First of all, I want to thank all of you for your hard work. It's because of your efforts that we've had such a profitable year." At the exit, Margaret held up a card reading, TEN MINUTES!!! Howard caught her eye and winked as he continued. "Tomorrow's Christmas Eve, so I want you to get some rest. But not too much." Chuckles bubbled in the crowd. "Because right after the holiday, we've got to get right back to work." Howard's fist shot into the air. "Harder than ever! Let's make Langston Mattresses number one!" A cheer grew. "Remember out motto: They snooze, we win. You snooze, we lose!"

The floor exploded into cheers and toasting. Howard allowed himself to be swarmed until he saw Margaret standing by the door, anxiously pointing at her watch. Then he plowed through the crowd to leave the room.

Margaret passed him his briefcase as he sailed by. "You're not going to make it," she said.

"I'm gonna make it!" echoed down the hallway as Howard raced from the building.

Howard wove his gleaming green Suburban through the busy Christmas Eve street traffic. With the skill of an Indy 500 racer, he dodged snarls, squeaked through narrow openings, and plowed ahead of less assertive drivers, making it to the freeway in record time. But Howard's triumph didn't last. His jaw nearly hit his chest when he crested the on-ramp and saw the freeway.

It looked like a parking lot.

Howard inched his way along the freeway as fast as he could, changing lanes in hopes of finding one that was moving faster than the others. But true to the rule, as soon as he was in a lane, all the others seemed to move faster. Howard ground his teeth in frustration.

Then he spotted the emergency lane. The empty emergency lane. Howard's face lit up.

He wrenched the Suburban over into the emergency lane and roared past the creeping commuters. *I'm gonna make it,* Howard thought, grinning.

Howard's grin bent into an angry scowl when flashing red lights appeared in his rearview mirror. He slowed the car to a stop resentfully and waited for the motorcycle cop to park his bike and walk up.

All starch and knife-edge creases, the cop loomed over Howard. "License and registration, please," he drawled.

Howard handed over his ID with a strained smile. "Look, Officer . . ." His eyes flicked to the name tag. "Hummell, I'm in kind of a hurry. I'm late for my son's karate class."

Officer Hummell looked horrified. "Oh, I *do* apologize if I've caused you some sort of delay. How thoughtless of me. Won't you please tell me how I can make it up to you?" He placed one palm to his chest. "Because the last thing I want on my conscience right now is a private citizen somehow dissatisfied with the performance of my duty." He sighed heavily. "I know I just wouldn't be able to sleep a wink tonight if that were indeed the case."

If Howard could have sunk into the bucket seat and disappeared, he would have. "No, I—I wasn't criticizing your—" he stammered. "I mean, I just got hung up at my office, and—"

"Oh, the office!" interrupted Hummell. He smiled

conspiratorially. "The employee Christmas party, perhaps? How nice. Spiked cider, eggnog, *wassail—*" His face hardened. "Step out of the car."

"What?" Howard was dumbfounded. "But . . . but . . . I haven't been drinking."

"Of *course* you haven't," snapped the cop. "And you weren't just driving seventy-five miles an hour in a safety lane either."

Howard sighed and got out of the car.

Across town, Jamie Langston tugged his white *gi* into position and marched out into the karate academy's auditorium with the rest of his class. He shot a glance up at the bleachers, packed with enthusiastic parents, siblings, and friends. His eye found his mother smiling and waving at him, then fell on the empty seat next to her. Jamie turned his head forward and tried to pretend he hadn't looked, but his friend Johnny Maltin nudged him in the ribs. Turning involuntarily, Jamie saw Johnny's father, Ted, sitting next to his mother and recording the event with his video camera. Jamie faked a smile and managed a limp wave before fixing his eyes rigidly in front again.

"Walk the line," Officer Hummell ordered.

Howard carefully placed one foot in front of the other under the motorcycle cop's hawkish scrutiny. "There. Are we finished?" He frowned at Hummell. "You've made me walk the line. You've made me touch my nose. You've made me walk the line *while* touching my nose! Are we finished?"

"Recite the alphabet," snapped Hummell. "Backward."

Howard finally screeched the Suburban to a halt directly in front of the doors to the karate academy. He barreled into the building and raced down the hall to the auditorium.

It was silent, a lone janitor slowly sweeping the floor. Howard clenched his fists.

He hadn't made it after all.

3

Howard Langston's black mood did not improve when he pulled up into his driveway to find his neighbor Ted Maltin hanging Christmas lights up on the Langston roof. Ted lived next door and always tried to be helpful, but it was the kind of helpful that had always set Howard's teeth on edge.

"Hey, neighbor!" called Ted from the roof. With a flourish, he plugged a wire into an extension cord. Cheery lights twinkled across the Langston roof, joining those of the rest of the neighborhood.

Howard gaped in openmouthed surprise as Ted climbed down the ladder from the roof. "I had some extra lights in the garage," said Ted. "And since you didn't put up any yourself, I figured, 'What the hey!' " He grinned expansively at Howard. "Why not spread some Christmas cheer around the neighborhood?"

"Gee, Ted. How . . . thoughtful," said Howard sarcastically.

Busy folding up the ladder, Ted missed the barb completely. He looked up at Howard with an expression of deep sadness. "Hey, sorry we missed you at the karate class today." Ted's frown switched to a smile as he clapped Howard on the shoulder. "But don't worry. I got it all on video for you."

Ted shouldered the ladder and headed back next door. Howard glowered after him. "What would I do without you?" he said dryly.

Howard found Liz emptying the dishwasher in the kitchen. "Did you tell Ted he could put lights on our house?" he barked by way of hello.

Liz glared up at her husband, anger heating her cheeks. "Do you have any idea what time it is?"

Howard withered under that glare. "I know." He sighed. "But you should have seen the traffic. And then of course I got a ticket and—"

Liz cut him off abruptly. "Don't explain it to *me*," she huffed. "It wasn't *my* karate class that you missed." She turned back to the dishwasher.

After a moment, Howard left the kitchen and headed for the living room.

"Hey, buddy," Howard greeted Jamie.

Jamie didn't look away from the TV screen, where a commercial for the Turbo Man action figure promised endless enjoyment and peer acceptance.

"Jamie," Howard began. "About your class tonight, I—"

Jamie switched off the TV and stomped into the kitchen. "Jamie?" Howard called after him. When no answer came, Howard followed his son into the kitchen.

Howard watched as Jamie got a juice box out of the refrigerator, yanking the door open and then slamming it shut. Jamie stalked directly past Howard without looking at him and ran upstairs. Howard shot a frustrated look at Liz, who shook her head and turned away without a word.

When he topped the stairs, Howard tapped gently on Jamie's bedroom door. "Jamie? Can I come in?" Silence followed. Howard opened the door and stepped inside.

Jamie sat on his bed, overintently reading a *Turbo Man* comic book. Howard feinted and jabbed at the empty air. "Hey, kiddo. Are those hands registered weapons yet?" Howard asked cheerily.

Jamie hadn't said a word to his father yet, but Howard was a salesman who never gave up on a pitch. He spied the purple belt draped over the back of a chair and hefted it with overstated wonder. "Wow! Is this it?"

Howard tied the belt around his forehead like a samurai warrior. He grinned at Jamie. "Does it go like this?" Howard struck a clownish kung fu pose, sawing the air and bleating fighting shouts. "How 'bout like this?"

When Jamie still didn't respond, Howard sighed heavily, dragged a kid-size chair over, and sat down next to his son. "I did something really stupid today, huh?"

Almost under his breath, Jamie answered, "I don't care."

"Aw, Jame. I hope that's not true," Howard said sincerely. "Because I really wanted to be there. Believe me."

Jamie finally looked up at his father. "But you *always* say that," he moaned. "And you never come anyway."

Howard sat back on his tiny chair and looked seriously at his son. "You're right. I blew it. And I'm really sorry. You think maybe you could let me make it up to you?"

"Like how?"

"Well . . ." Howard pondered. "How 'bout letting me do something special. Just for you. Like if there's something really important you've been wanting for Christmas?"

Jamie shrugged at the offer. "Oh. I already wrote Santa a letter. He'll get it for me."

Howard coughed into his hand. "Well, Santa can get *very* busy this time of year. And sometimes he asks Moms and Dads to help out a little. So if there's a special present you really want, maybe *I* could get it for you so Santa can concentrate on everything else."

Jamie returned to his comic book. "Nah, it's not *that* important," he said offhandedly. "You're probably busier than Santa, anyway."

"I'm not *that* busy." Howard laughed. "C'mon. Tell me. What do you want?"

Jamie's eyes lit up. "I want the Turbo Man action figure with the arms and legs that move and the Boomerang Shooter and the Rockin' Roarin' Jet Pack and the realistic voice-activator that says five different phrases, including 'It's Turbo Time,' with accessories sold separately, batteries not included!"

"Glad you had to stop and think about it." Howard smiled.

"Johnny-next-door's gonna get one and so'll everybody else I know." Jamie looked up at Howard. "Whoever doesn't will be a real *loser.*"

"Well, that definitely won't be you," Howard said emphatically.

"Really?"

"Don't worry, son." Howard shot Jamie his most forcefully sincere look. "You can count on me."

Jamie's face filled with pleasure. He hugged Howard. "I love you, Dad."

Touched, Howard replied softly, "I love you, too, Jamie."

"It's not like I do it on purpose!" snapped Howard, wiping his face with a towel as he entered the bedroom.

"I know you don't, Howard." Liz sighed, looking up

from the package she was wrapping on the bed. "But how many excuses am I supposed to make for you? I mean, when was the last time you spent any real time with us?" She knitted her brows together. "As a *family.*"

Howard groped for a moment, then shot back, "We went to Hawaii last summer."

"Yeah," said Liz, pursing her lips. "And you spent the entire time trying to convince everybody to buy new mattresses from you."

"What about the boat tour," objected Howard. "We did *that* together. And that was a great time! Jamie *still* talks about that day!"

"Exactly," pounced Liz. "That *day*. One day, Howard. Out of our entire vacation, we come back with *one* day worth remembering." She tied a bow on the package. "One day."

Howard looked hurt. "I just want you and Jamie to have the best of everything. Why else do you think I work so hard."

Liz looked at her husband straightforwardly. "Because you can't help it." She held up her hand to quell Howard's objection. "You're the most competitive person I know. I mean, look at your motto: You snooze, you lose . . ."

"I don't say that!" Howard was emphatic. "It's *they* snooze, we win. You snooze, we lose!"

"Whatever," Liz said. "I know how important success is to you. I know how important *winning* is to you." She paused. "I'd just like to know how important *we* are to you."

Howard put his hands on his wife's shoulders. "You're very important to me."

Liz shrugged out of his grip. "I'm your number one customer," she said dryly. She walked to the middle of the bedroom and spread her arms. "I love everything you've done for us. The cars, the vacations, this house—they're all wonderful. But they're so much better if *you're* around to enjoy them *with* us!"

Liz faced Howard and put her hands on his shoulders. "I love you, Howard. Jamie loves you. But he needs more than just *one* day. He needs to know he can depend on you. That you'll keep your promises. That you'll be there with the other dads." Liz let go of him and walked into the bathroom.

Howard stood in the bedroom, feeling hurt and annoyed. "You mean like Ted?" he snapped. "Mister Got-It-All-on-Video? Sure, I guess if I sued my company for chronic migraines due to . . . what was it?"

"Toner fumes from the copy machine," called out Liz.

"Right." Howard scowled. "Then I could stay home all day."

"You're missing the point," said Liz as she turned out the bathroom light and returned to the bedroom. "I don't want you to be more like Ted. I just want you to be a little more focused on your son. Jamie's only going to be a kid once. I don't think you want to miss that."

Howard settled into his side of the bed. "I'm not," he told his wife. "I mean, you should have seen us in there just now. We were really bonding. Talking about Turbo Guy—"

"Turbo Man," corrected Liz as she slid into her side of the bed. "That reminds me. You got the doll, right?"

Howard looked at her in confusion. "The doll?"

Liz fluffed up her pillow. "The Turbo Man doll," she said around a yawn. "I asked you to pick one up. Two weeks ago."

"Oh." Howard made a sour face. *"That* doll."

Liz turned to stare at her husband with dismay. "Oh, Howard! You didn't. I can't believe you forgot!"

"What?" Howard batted his eyes in confusion. "No. I didn't forget. I got it." He recovered smoothly. He closed his eyes and snuggled down into the pillow. "The Turbo Man doll. With the thing that shoots . . . and the rockem-sockem jet pack." A yawn halted him for a second. "And the realistic voice box that says, 'It's Turbo Time.' Of course, I got the doll."

"Good," said Liz, rolling over and putting out the light. "Because at this point, they'd probably be impossible to find."

In the dark, Howard's eyes snapped open.

4

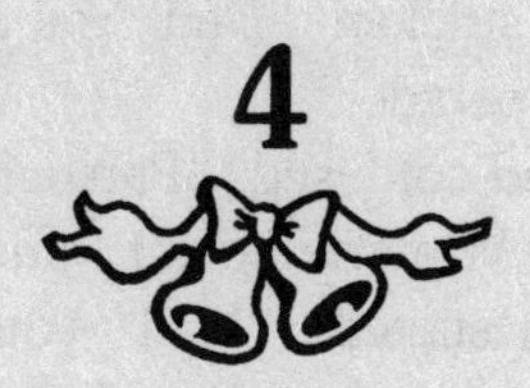

It seemed to Howard that he had closed his eyes for only a moment. He was confused by the bright sunlight streaming in the bedroom window. Wearily, he looked at the clock on his nightstand. It read 8:05.

Howard bolted out of bed and grabbed for his clothes.

Liz and Jamie were chatting merrily over breakfast, still in their pajamas, when Howard came barreling into the kitchen, fully dressed. Liz shot him a questioning glance as he kissed her good morning. "Where are you going?" she asked with surprise.

"I've got to run to the office," Howard muttered under his breath.

"Howard! It's Christmas Eve!" Liz yelped. Her lips thinned. "You are *not* going to the office!"

Howard leaned close to whisper in his wife's ear. "I have to pick up the D-O-L-L. I left it there by mistake."

Jamie looked stricken. "Dad! You can't go to work! What about the parade?"

Howard looked confused. "Parade?"

"The Holiday Wintertainment Parade! We go every year!" Jamie hesitated. "Well, you didn't go last year . . . or the year before. But Mom and I always go." He looked plaintively at his father. "Anyway, this year Turbo Man's gonna be there and it's gonna be really cool. You can't miss it, Dad."

Howard put his hands on Jamie's shoulders and looked him straight in the eye. "Hey," he said. "I won't miss it. I'll be there."

Liz said, "He'll be right back." She pointed a finger at Howard. "Won't you?"

Howard gave her his broadest grin. "I'll be an hour, tops. I promise."

And with a wave, he was out the door.

Howard was standing in his driveway, about to open the car door, when he heard an odd grunting noise behind him. When he turned to look, he found a live reindeer charging at him. Howard was a big man, but the reindeer was much bigger. He yanked the door open and dove into the car.

The reindeer's head was inches from his own when the animal was suddenly jerked to a halt. Howard's shock subsided enough for him to notice that the reindeer had a collar on. A leash ran from the collar to a wind-up reel in the hands of Howard's neighbor Ted.

Ted trotted forward, reeling in the leash as he came. "Sorry about that, Howie," Ted said cheerfully.

Howard looked at Ted in disbelief. "Is that a reindeer?"

"Little Christmas surprise for my boy, Johnny," Ted beamed.

Howard tried to smile. "How touching." He reached a hand out to pet the reindeer's nose but snatched it back as the animal growled and snapped at his fingers.

"That's odd," said Ted, puzzled. "Reindeer are usually such gentle animals. Must be something about you that he doesn't like. Aftershave or something?"

"Yeah," said Howard, closing the door and starting the car. "Anyway, gotta go."

Ted missed the hint, as usual. He leaned on the door. "Where you off to so early?" he asked.

"Just picking up a Christmas present. For Jamie." Howard's hopes of a quick getaway faded.

"Oh-ho!" Ted's laugh boomed across the yard. "Nothing like waiting until the last minute! What'cha gettin' him?"

"One of those Turbo Mans."

Ted punched Howard lightly on the arm. "Hey! That's great!" Ted grinned. "I got a Turbo Man for Johnny *months* ago! It's nestled safely under our tree."

Howard had had enough. He started backing the car out of the driveway. But Ted wasn't done yet. As

Howard moved away, he called out, "Oh, Howard! They say it may get icy later. Maybe you should wrap some chains around your tires."

Howard pulled out into the street. "Maybe I should wrap some chains around you," he growled as he sped away.

When Howard parked in the lot of the TOYS! TOYS! TOYS! store he was shocked to see a huge mob of people crowded against the still-closed doors. He dove into the rear of the crowd and slowly muscled his way to the front.

Inside the glass doors of the store, Howard could see a weaselly clerk swinging a key on a chain. He looked as if he was whistling. Howard knocked on the door to get the clerk's attention, but Weasel Face made a great show of ignoring Howard.

"Don't bother," said a voice next to him. "It's only eight fifty-eight, and he won't open the doors before the nine o'clock opening time. Enough to drive a man insane, ain't it?"

Howard turned to look at the man who had spoken. It was a stocky man in a post office uniform, complete with a bulging mail sack that bumped several people as the mailman turned to face Howard. The man seemed grumpy and irritable, and his eyes had an unnerving glint to them, but he stuck out his hand toward Howard. "Myron Larrabee," he said.

Howard's salesman reflexes had him shaking Larrabee's hand without thinking. "Howard Langston," he replied.

"Last-minute shopping, huh?"

"Yeah," grunted Howard, turning back to the glass doors.

Myron plowed on without noticing. "Me, I got no choice," he declared. "Busiest time of the year. Gotta move all those important Christmas cards from people who never even speak to each other during the rest of the year. Then there are the presents from relatives that'll probably get returned anyway." Howard turned back as the mailman continued to complain. "Not to mention all the stinkin' letters to 'Santa at the North Pole.' 'Course, we just send those straight to the furnace."

A little boy next to Myron began to cry. His father moved him away, telling the terror-stricken boy, "He didn't mean that, son. He was only joking." The man glared at the mailman and hissed, "Moron!"

"That's *Myron!"* snapped Myron. He waved a finger as the boy and his father retreated. "I know where you live, pal!" Myron turned back to Howard. "See why I hate Christmas?"

"Sounds like you have a tough job," said Howard soothingly.

Myron's eyes lit up dangerously. "I can handle it," he said defensively. "You think I can't handle it?"

"I didn't say that." Howard wanted no trouble.

"As if I didn't already have enough pressure," Myron

went on. "My kid sent me out here for some goofy toy. Some fruity robot called Turtle Man."

"You mean Turbo Man," Howard corrected.

"Yeah, him," agreed Myron.

"My kid wants one, too."

Myron leaned close to Howard and said in a low voice, "If you ask me, it's all a ploy."

"A ploy?"

"You know," said Myron conspiratorially. "Created by rich and powerful toy cartels. A bunch of fat cats taking advantage of us poor workin' stiffs. They advertise all over TV. Create this frenzy. Use *subliminal messages* to make every kid in America think he's a worthless piece of garbage if his daddy doesn't buy him some cheap little plastic toy."

If Howard could have moved away, he would have. But the crowd pressed him close to Myron, and Myron, it seemed, was just getting warmed up. "Oh, I'd like to get my hands on one of those guys," he said, his meaty hands clenching and unclenching. "Squeeze his soft, pink little neck until his beady little eyeballs pop right out of their sockets. Then I'd take his bloated body and—" Myron stopped suddenly, as if he'd realized that he'd gone too far. He tried to smile offhandedly. "I'm just saying it's unfair. To us workin' stiffs. You know?"

Howard was saved from having to say more than "Right" by the jingle of the clerk's key in the lock. The door opened and Howard was carried bodily into the store by the press of the crowd, which poured inward like water from a bursting dam.

Shoppers climbed over each other in their rush to get to various aisles. Howard saw a man trip and fall. The man's wife turned back for him. The downed man clutched at his leg in pain but waved his wife on. "No!" he shouted. "Go on without me!" The crowd swallowed him up, but his voice could still be heard. "The Malibu Barbie Dream House! The Malibu Barbie—"

Howard didn't hear any more. He and Myron raced down the aisle, dodging around parents who were already pulling toys off shelves. Ahead, Howard could see the top of a towering Turbo Man display. A shopper toppled a rack of plush toys right in front of him and he just barely cleared the fuzzy hazard with a mighty leap. He jolted to a stop directly in front of the Turbo Man display.

It was empty.

Howard was stunned. "The Turbo Man dolls! They're all gone!" he cried.

Myron appeared beside him. "They can't be!"

Howard snagged the sleeve of a hapless clerk who was trying to swim upstream toward the front of the store. "I'm trying to find a Turbo Man!"

"Me, too," chimed in Myron.

The clerk stared at the two men for a moment and then burst into laughter. "Hey, Ronnie!" he shouted to a co-worker. "These guys are looking for a Turbo Man!"

To Howard's consternation, the co-worker began laughing hysterically, too. "Hey, everybody!" Ronnie shouted to the other shoppers. "These two guys are looking for a Turbo Man!"

Almost as one, all the shoppers crammed into the toy store began laughing. People slapped each other on the back and cackled, "They're looking for a Turbo Man!"

The first sales clerk finally recovered enough to gasp at Howard and Myron. "Where have you guys been? Turbo Man's been the biggest seller of the season!"

Ronnie smirked as he added, "You got a better chance of being crowned Miss America than you do of finding a Turbo Man!"

"Especially on Christmas Eve!" called out someone from the crowd of shoppers.

The sales clerk waved at a nearby pile of plush saber-toothed tiger dolls that obviously hadn't been disturbed for weeks. "We've got plenty of Turbo Man's pal, Booster, though." This brought another round of wild laughter from everyone.

Except from Howard and Myron, that is. Howard lost his patience. He grabbed each clerk by his collar and lifted them both effortlessly up to eye level. "Where's your Christmas spirit?" he growled quietly, dangerously.

The mocking merriment vanished from the clerks' faces, replaced by earnest please-don't-hurt-me smiles.

Howard lowered them both gently. "Now, there

must be a Turbo Man around here somewhere," he suggested with careful emphasis.

The clerks looked at each other. "Actually . . ." began Ronnie, "the last one left a minute ago. Some short lady had it on layaway."

"Short lady? What short lady?" barked Howard and Myron in unison.

The first clerk pointed toward the front of the store. "In a fur coat," he said. "She's probably leaving about now."

Without warning, Myron slammed Howard in the chest with the bulging mail sack, knocking Howard backward into a display of sporting goods. Myron raced toward the front doors as Howard disappeared under a pile of basketballs and celebrity-endorsed shorts.

Myron didn't get far, however. His foot came down on a radio-controlled car as it sped unexpectedly between his legs, and the mailman went down. Howard threw off the sports gear and raced out of the store.

Outside the toy store, Howard spotted a short middle-aged woman in a fur coat at the corner of the street, waiting for the light to change. She clutched a large TOYS! TOYS! TOYS! bag tightly to her chest.

Howard sprinted over to her and grabbed her by the upper arm. The woman let out a shriek. "What do you want?"

Gasping for breath, Howard began, "I followed you from the store—"

"Oh?" said the woman, her eyebrows rising in interest.

"I want to offer you *twice* what you paid for your bag," said Howard, pointing at the gaudy plastic container.

"My b-bag?" stuttered the woman. "Twice?"

"Okay," said Howard hurriedly. *"Three* times!"

The woman blinked in surprise. "Oh. Well," she said, "for that kind of profit, knock yourself out."

Howard pressed a wad of cash into her hand and took charge of the bag. The woman left quickly, smiling and shaking her head.

Howard opened the bag and looked inside . . .

. . . to see a fluffy pink Booster doll.

Howard angrily threw the doll in a nearby trash can and looked around for the short woman in the fur coat. She went speeding by him in a station wagon, a Turbo Man doll propped up in the back window as though it was waving at Howard.

Howard ran down the street after the station wagon but was rapidly left behind. He collapsed heavily onto a bus stop bench to catch his breath. Only after he'd sat down did he notice that the bench's ad displayed a saluting Turbo Man, urging people to attend the Holiday Wintertainment Parade. Howard's eyes burned into the illustration.

"This is war!"

5

That glimpse of Turbo Man in the back of the station wagon was as close as Howard got to the doll for the rest of the morning.

At store after store across town, the situation was the same: Howard would go into a toy store, ask for a Turbo Man doll, then burn with humiliation as each and every shop clerk laughed in his face. Oh, some were nicer than others—managing to merely snicker and jiggle with suppressed merriment—but most took a malicious glee in pointing out to anyone within earshot that another sucker had missed the boat on the hottest toy of the year.

Every failure was compounded by the scrutiny of hundreds of Turbo Man ads and posters. As the centerpiece and star attraction of the Holiday Wintertainment Parade, the action hero's stern mask sneered at Howard from nearly every shop window and bus bench. As an insulting afterthought, nearly every empty Turbo Man display was accompanied by a huge stack of obviously nonselling Booster dolls.

Hours had gone by, and Howard had progressed from the major toy stores to the tawdry Z-Mart chains in his desperate search when he finally lost it. In a tiny hole-in-the-mall store his hopes were raised by a clerk who didn't laugh when Howard tiredly asked for a Turbo Man. The pimply teenager just jerked a thumb toward the back of the store without looking up from his portable TV. Howard ran down the aisle only to find yet another set of empty shelves fronted by an inflated Turbo Man stand-up. The store hadn't even bothered to stock the Boosters.

The Turbo Man stand-up seemed to mock Howard, smiling and waving an automated arm at him. Fed up with frustration, Howard launched a mighty right cross at the stand-up, laying it flat on its back. But the display was weighted at the bottom, and when Howard spun on his heel to leave, the stand-up snapped upright again, slamming into the back of Howard's head.

Liz Langston was dusted with a light coating of flour, and splotches of food coloring spotted her clothes like cheery polka dots. With practiced ease, she opened the oven and swapped the sheet with unbaked cookies with the hot one laden with golden brown disks. She slid the warm cookies out onto a dish to cool next to the dozens of others covering the table. The rich smell of baking filled the kitchen. From the living room came the sounds of Jamie and Johnny at play. Behind Liz, the back door opened and Ted walked in. "Hi, Liz," he called, brushing off his hands, "I was shoveling my walk, and I noticed a nasty patch of ice by your garage door. I didn't want anyone to slip, so I put down some rock salt."

"Thanks, Ted," said Liz, turning back to the counter and rolling out dough for the next batch of cookies.

Ted stood for a moment, looking around the kitchen. Spotting an open cabinet door, he closed it. It made a squeaking sound, so he opened and closed it a couple of times. "Hmm," he said to Liz. "Does this squeaking bother you? I could take care of it with some WD-40."

Liz glanced over at the door uncertainly. "Well . . . sure. If you want to."

Ted smiled and moved close to Liz, watching her as she cut out another batch of cookies with a Santa-shaped cutter. "Look at you," he said. "It's Christmas Eve and you're slaving over a hot stove. Is this the Mom of the Year or what?" He smiled at her and winked.

"It's no big deal," said Liz as she lifted the cookies, slid past Ted, and performed the pan switch with the oven again.

Ted moved closer. "And modest, too."

Liz took a moment to blot her forehead with a towel. When she looked up, Ted was standing right in front of her.

"Why, Liz, you're all flushed." Ted reached out and gently took the oven mitts off Liz's hands. "Looks like you could use a little 'you' time," he said, smiling. "Why don't you go upstairs? Take a shower. Relax. I'll keep an eye on the boys. Finish up the cookies."

Liz recognized that Ted's "helpfulness" would not be politely avoidable. "Okay," she said with a sigh, untying her apron. "But listen for the oven timer. The cookies—"

"I know," interrupted Ted. "Sugar cookies. Oven at three fifty. Bake for twelve to fifteen minutes until golden brown." He took the apron from her and tied it on, oblivious to the silly picture he made. "Ted's got everything under control."

Liz watched as Ted took a spatula and started making artful arrangements of finished cookies on a plate. She shook her head in disbelief and headed on upstairs.

The long bank of pay phones facing the street were all occupied by harried father types all frustrated by their inability to find a simple doll and all trying to explain this on Christmas Eve to unsympathetic family members.

"I didn't say I *couldn't* get the doll! I just said I may be a little late . . ."

"But, sweetie, you wouldn't believe how *hard* these things are to find . . ."

"No, no! I'll *get* it! I may have to go out of state, but I'll *get* it!"

At the last pay phone, Howard reluctantly dialed his home number. He inhaled deeply as it rang.

"Merry Christmas! Langston residence!"

"Hi, I—" The air whooshed out of Howard. "Ted—?"

"Howard! Hey, buddy!" said Ted brightly. "How you doin' out there? Everything okay?"

Howard ground his molars. "Yeah, fine. Look, I need to speak to Liz. Could you—"

The sound of crunching mixed with Ted's reply. "Mmm! Oh, Howard! Excuse me . . . your wife's cookies are out of this world!"

"What are you—Who said you could eat my cookies?"

"I was just helping Liz out a little in the kitchen. She's baking up a storm here."

"Ted, I need to speak to my wife. Please put Liz on the phone."

"I think she's in the shower, Howard. Do you want me to go up and check?"

"NO!" Howard controlled himself quickly. "I mean, no, that's fine. *On your way out,* tell her I'm going to be a few minutes late, but she shouldn't worry."

"Oh, she won't worry. I mean, I'm here, and—" Another crunching sound. "Oh, wow! Ummm! These cookies! I've *gotta* get the recipe from Liz!"

"Put that cookie down!" yelled Howard. *"Now!"*

"Howard? Is something bothering you?" Ted asked with some concern. "Because this time of year there's a very high incidence of stress-related breakdowns. You may want to try some deep-breathing exercises or—" A ding sounded faintly behind Ted's voice. "Oops! There's the next batch! Sorry, Howard, gotta go. I'll give Liz your message, though. Take care, buddy."

The phone clicked dead in Howard's ear. Angrily, he slammed the handset back into its cradle.

"Well, look who it is," came a voice from over Howard's shoulder. Howard spun to his left. "Still on the hunt?" asked Myron Larrabee, standing at the next phone.

Howard acknowledged the mailman with a thin smile and then moved away from the telephones.

Myron followed him. "Sorry 'bout whackin' ya back at that toy store. I guess I let the spirit of friendly competition get to me."

Howard kept walking. "It's no problem. Really."

Myron seemed to have a point to make. He zipped ahead of Howard. "I figured you woulda done the same thing. Which makes me realize we're pretty much the same kinda guys, you an' me."

Howard sped up his pace. "I sort of doubt that . . ."

But Myron was not about to be left behind. He matched Howard's pace and continued earnestly, "And with all this brouhaha happenin' over the doll, well, I was thinking what a great team we'd make. Go after Turbo Man as a *unit.* You know, join forces, divide and conquer, search and destroy! Whaddaya say?"

Howard had made it to his car and was patting his

pockets in search of his keys. "Thanks, Myron, but I really don't think—"

"C'mon, man," Myron interrupted. "Let's do it! Let's be a team!"

Howard looked up at the mailman's face, at the flushed expression, the too-bright eyes. He spoke soothingly. "Gee, Myron. I think you're really a good guy and all . . . I just think this is something I'd . . . like to do myself. You understand, right?"

Myron pulled himself up straight and stared at Howard through slitted eyes. "Oh, I understand *plenty!*" he snarled. "Sure. You with your fancy car and fancy shoes. I'm good enough to talk to in *line,* but I'm not good enough to be on your *team*—is that it?"

"No, that's not what I'm saying," began Howard.

A wild-eyed man suddenly ran past them, shouting, "Toy Works just got a last-minute delivery of Turbo Mans!"

Howard and Myron locked eyes.

Both men sprinted for their cars. Myron made it to his postal Jeep first. In a smooth maneuver, he backed it up and peeled out into the street. Howard was a second behind Myron. He fired up the Suburban and threw it into reverse—and plowed into a parked police motorcycle, which toppled over and landed with the sharp sound of breaking glass. Howard grimaced, looked into his rearview mirror, then hung his head.

He heard the *toc-toc-toc* of approaching boots.

When they stopped by the window, Howard looked up at the cop and his heart sank.

"You broke my little mirror," said Officer Hummell. "License and registration."

Twenty minutes later, Howard dove into the pulsing river of desperate consumers that clogged every square foot in the Mall of America. Even with his bulk and aggressive attitude, it took him quite a while to get to the doors of Toy Works.

The inside of Toy Works was even more crowded than the mall, if that was possible. As he elbowed his way up to the front counter, Howard saw Myron thrashing away nearby. When no more bodies could be pushed in any direction, Howard stopped trying to get any farther.

Behind the counter, a ring of employees parted to reveal a pimply store manager standing unsteadily on a child's plastic chair. He raised a toy megaphone to his lips and addressed the crowd. "Listen up, people, 'cause I'm only gonna say this once."

The crowd hushed.

"Now, to answer your first question: Yes, the rumors are true. We *have* received a small quantity of the action figures known as Turbo Man—" The manager's reedy voice was drowned out by a cheer from the crowd of anxious shoppers. He reddened and barked at them, "I'm not going to ask you people for quiet again! Do you understand me?"

The crowd hushed again.

"Here's how things are going to work." The manager made a sweeping gesture toward the wall with his free hand. "You will all form an orderly line so that an employee can hand you a *numbered ball.* The balls will then be drawn in a standard lottery fashion to see who gets a doll."

The crowd murmured excitedly, surging over to where the line would form.

"I'd like to add that if you're *not* one of the lucky few, we do have plenty of Turbo Man's faithful pet tiger, Booster, in stock."

This brought a scattering of boos from the crowd.

"Oh, and by the way," the manager said, drunk with his new power, "in accordance with the laws of supply and demand, the new list price for each figure has just *doubled!*"

This brought more boos from the crowd, but people generally behaved and started forming a line. Two vacant-eyed teenagers began to slowly pass out numbered Ping-Pong balls from a box on the counter.

Howard groaned at the snail-like pace of the distribution. He decided to see if there was something he could do to speed the process up. Pumping himself up into full salesman mode, he strode up to the young manager, smiled and extended his hand. "Hi," he boomed heartily. "Howard Langston. Nice to meet you."

"What?" said the manager, still speaking through his megaphone.

Howard tried to gently push the megaphone aside and speak confidentially to the teenager. "You look like an enterprising young man. What do you say you go in the back, set aside a Turbo Man doll for me, and we work out some kind of *compensation?*"

The manager kept the megaphone locked to his lips. "Sir . . . are you trying to bribe me?" The crowd heard this quite clearly and began to growl at Howard. The megaphone zoomed in on Howard. "Get to the back of the line!" the manager thundered.

Howard backed away from the counter toward the line. Somebody shook a fist at him as he walked by, then someone took a swing. In a flash, order disappeared and the bodies surged forward. The box with the numbered Ping-Pong balls flew high in the air, scattering small white orbs over the crowd. The surge became a free-for-all as everyone scrambled for the bouncing balls.

Howard followed a white blur as it headed for the door. He launched a flying tackle at the ball and landed in a heap just outside the Toy Works store. Almost afraid to look, Howard opened his clutched hand.

It was there. He had the ball!

Suddenly a hand clamped onto Howard's wrist. Howard tried to wrench his hand free but wound up tumbling backward, bumping off bodies on his way down but pulling his attacker with him. It was Myron.

The mailman pried the ball out of Howard's fingers

and heaved himself to his feet. "It's mine!" Myron crowed.

Howard was pinned to the floor by a moving forest of legs and so couldn't free himself to chase Myron. He did the next best thing by pointing at Myron and shouting at the top of his lungs, "Hey, *everybody*! He took *two!*"

Like sharks catching the scent of blood in the water, the crowd spun in place and lunged at the hapless mailman. Howard smiled grimly as Myron sank into a whirlpool of clawing hands and thumping fists.

His smile changed to genuine pleasure as he saw a white Ping-Pong ball bobble out from the crowd of legs and bounce its way into the mall. No one else appeared to see the ball escape. Howard's pleasure swelled to a fierce joy as he scrambled after the round prize.

Had Howard been possessed of a scientific turn of mind, the next few minutes might have been an endlessly fascinating study in physics—covering ballistics, probability patterns, the ever-changing velocity of an elastic sphere as it collided with various obstacles and rebounded in a completely unpredictable manner. But being a simple salesman, what Howard saw was a Ping-Pong ball with an evil sense of humor.

The ball led Howard on a merry chase through the mall. It managed to bounce along the tile floor without being crushed by the shuffling legs of hundreds of shoppers. Those same legs turned into an impassable forest when Howard dove after the ball—a forest that kicked, swore, and brutally stomped his seeking fingers. But Howard kept going after that ball, jostling everybody enough that men, women, and even kids threw the joyous Christmas spirit out the window and yelled at him.

Howard caught a glimpse of the ball as it *ponked* once on the metal plate at the top of an escalator and then disappeared over the edge of the first tread. He shoved his way down the up escalator until the outraged crowd fought him to a standstill. In desperation, he vaulted over the side, hoping the floor wasn't *too* far below.

Fortunately, it wasn't. Howard landed with a brain-jarring jolt, but he managed to stay on his feet. *There!* The ball was bouncing through an elaborate display of Lego toys! Without thinking, Howard dove after it. Multicolored Lego blocks exploded in a fountain of plastic as he plowed through the display, kicking pieces out of his way, tripping over other pieces and completely toppling a giant Lego castle. Like a madman, he tried to catch the Ping-Pong ball, but it bounced out of the store and right up to the edge of the walkway.

Howard launched himself in a flying tackle, but all he gained was a closer view of the ball as it fell from his level down into a baby stroller on the first floor. The toddler in the stroller burbled in delight at this gift from heaven and immediately stuck the Ping-Pong ball in his mouth.

Keeping an eye on the toddler, Howard sidled along the walkway until he came to a glass-sided elevator. It was jammed with shoppers who spilled out onto the walkway as the doors opened. More shoppers rushed in, carrying Howard forward until his face was smushed against the glass.

Everyone left the elevator in an explosive rush when it opened on the ground floor. Over bobbing heads, Howard saw the toddler's mother push the stroller into the children's play area, a maze of plastic tubes, jungle gyms, and a ball room.

Howard's heart sank as he saw the toddler, ball now clutched in his chubby hand, climb down from his stroller and crawl into the open mouth of the tube maze.

Like a giant hamster habitat, the tube maze twisted and turned on itself, climbing up in gentle stages to the top, where a single tube offered a thrilling slide-ride back down again. Howard crawled through the tight tubes after the toddler, ignoring the outraged reactions of parents and onlookers who shouted at him and pounded on the sides of the maze.

The toddler made it to the top of the maze before Howard and giggled happily as he slid down the long slide. Too far gone to stop now, Howard wormed his way onto the slide, shooting downward headfirst. He reached the bottom—and gasped.

He'd landed knee-deep in the ball room, a play pit filled with brightly colored rubber balls. Everywhere he looked there were balls—big balls, little balls, red balls, green balls, yellow balls, every color, every size, every-*where!*

Howard groaned.

Suddenly the toddler burst up out of the piled balls with squeals of glee. And miracle of miracles, he still had the Ping-Pong ball! It was clutched in his candy-sticky hand, but Howard didn't care. He cautiously approached the child, holding up a red ball. "Hi, little fella," he coaxed. "Look what I've got—a shiny *red* ball! Oooh! Do you want to trade?"

The ball disappeared into the small mouth. Howard got frantic. "No, no, no! Don't do that!" he pleaded. "You want something to eat? I'll buy you anything in the mall. Candy? Pretzel?" The kid wasn't responding. Howard reached for his sticky little mouth. "Why don't you just—" he started.

"Get away from my kid, you sicko!" screamed the toddler's mother. She clobbered Howard's head with her purse. She continued to smack him as she scooped her child up and dragged him out of the ball room.

Howard followed, trying to explain. "Lady, wait—!" But a crowd of enraged parents swarmed him as he left the ball room, shouting, "Pervert! Creep!" The last Howard saw of the Ping-Pong ball was when the toddler finally spit it out, where it disappeared beneath the feet of the latest flood of shoppers leaving the elevator.

Howard was busily banging his head against the plastic wall of the play room, hoping that applied pain would clear his head and maybe even wake him up from this nightmare, when a dry little voice whispered, "Psst! Buddy!"

The voice came from behind a tacky plywood cottage that had been sprayed with tacky artificial snow. Howard recognized it as the standard mall Santa's Cottage and was somehow not surprised that it was Santa himself who had called.

Well, make that a cut-rate Santa with a wrinkled uniform and a fake beard and eyebrows that threatened to peel off at any moment. Hovering around Santa's belt level was a sour-faced, middle-aged dwarf dressed as an elf.

As soon as he saw that he had Howard's attention, the Santa hissed again. "You wanna Turbo Man for Christmas?"

Howard stared at the Santa in disbelief. "Forget it," he sneered. "I'm not sitting on your lap."

The Santa looked equally scornful. "Hey, chief. I'm just a reputable businessman looking to give you a leg up out of that stinking pit you call life. But with your attitude, I don't think I wanna give you access to *this—*" He waved his hand and the elf thrust an instant photo at Howard. It was a lopsided portrait of the mall Santa holding a Turbo Man doll in one hand and a copy of the Christmas Eve edition of the newspaper in the other.

"Dat was taken dis morning," said the elf.

"Forget it, Tony," said Santa, pulling the elf's picture-holding arm back. "This guy doesn't want our help."

Howard held up his hand. "Wait. Hold on. We're all . . . businessmen." His salesman smile flashed charmingly. "I'm sure we can work out some sort of agreement."

Santa and the elf exchanged glances. Santa turned back to Howard. "You got the cash, we got the doll."

"How much?" said Howard, tugging at his wallet.

Santa looked shocked. "What, are you crazy?" he whispered, eyes darting left and right. "Santa *never* delivers a gift in broad daylight!"

Howard froze, which Santa took as agreement. "We can't talk here," he said, his fake beard slipping. "Let's go to your sleigh."

"My *what?*" asked Howard.

Santa pressed his drooping beard back on his cheek, but it wouldn't stick. "Your sleigh. Your *vehicle?*"

For Howard, the real world was long gone. He knew he was in Wonderland now. "Oh." He smiled. "Of course."

Tony the Elf was already tacking up an Out to Lunch sign on the cottage. "You got seat belts in the back?" he asked Howard over his shoulder.

Twenty minutes later, Howard pulled the Suburban up to the gate of a warehouse in the farthest section of town. The guard at the gate had a vicious-looking dog with reindeer antlers strapped to its head. Santa waved to the guard, who opened the gate and let the car in.

They parked before the steel door to the warehouse.

Santa got out of the car, walked to the door, and knocked with a strange rhythm. *TAP-tap-tap. TAP-tap-tap. TAP-TAP-tap-tap-TAP.* Howard recognized it as "Jingle Bells." Of course. The door opened and Howard was hustled quickly inside.

A hush spread through the enormous warehouse as twenty-odd Santas, a few Mrs. Clauses, and a large group of elves froze in position and stared at the newcomers. Howard's Santa said, "It's okay. He's cool." And the warehouse went back to work. Santas with humming forklifts moved pallets of toys from loading bays to the towering shelves that filled the great space. Elves scurried about with clipboards and pens, keeping count of the toys. Mrs. Clauses sat at tables neatly sorting stacks of cash. The place really looked like the stockroom of the North Pole.

Howard's Santa turned to his elf. "Tony. Get the man his Turbo Man."

Tony took off at a trot. Howard finally gave voice to the uneasiness that had been building up inside him. "Uh . . . Santa," he began. "I've got to tell you there's something here that doesn't seem quite . . . ethical."

"Ethical?" said Santa as he tugged at his semidetached beard. "This from a guy who tried to assault a toddler for a Ping-Pong ball." The beard came loose with a jerk, leaving a raw patch on Santa's face. "We're providing a service here. Us guys in the malls work hard this time of year. The pay stinks. We get every strain of virus and flu from the little tykes." He scratched at the raw spot. "Plus, every five minutes we're cleaning up *another* stain left by some baby on our knee. But the truth is, we're not doin' this for *us*—we're doin' it for the *kids.*"

Howard raised his eyebrows. "The kids?"

"For every one of 'em who ever sat down on Santa's lap," Santa declared with passion. "For the hundreds of dreams we hear every day, listening to all those kids tell us what they want. A certain game, a special doll—and in our hearts, we know that most of you idiots are too wrapped up in your jobs or marital problems to ever take note—to even *care!* The thought of those kids waking up Christmas morning without that special gift . . ." His voice cracked and he wiped a tear from his eye. "Just breaks my heart."

Howard stared at the Santa. "So where *does* all this stuff come from?"

Santa glared at Howard like a barracuda. "Who're you, the Question King?"

Tony the Elf arrived just then with a brand-new Turbo Man doll. Howard reached for it, but the Santa snatched it away first. He looked down his nose at Howard. "That'll be three hundred."

"Dollars?!" yipped Howard.

"No. Chocolate kisses," sneered Santa. *"Yes,* dollars!"

Howard's eyes narrowed. "What happened to all your lofty ideals? I thought you were *doing this for the kids!"*

"Sure." Santa shrugged. "But I don't see why we can't pick up a little loose change in the process."

"Loose change," grumbled Howard as he handed Santa the money. Santa smiled and handed Howard the doll. Howard examined the doll carefully and then gingerly pressed one of the buttons on its back.

Santa suddenly panicked. "No! Don't—!"

An authoritative electronic voice boomed out from the doll. In Korean.

Santa shot Howard a sickly smile and said lamely, "That's the *multilingual* version. It's . . . uh . . . fun and educational."

Howard threw the doll to the floor. "You're nothing but a bunch of sleazy con men in red suits!" he growled.

Santa's eyes widened in anger. "What'd you call us?"

"Con men," sneered Howard. "Thieves. Degenerates. Lowlifes. Scuzzy Santas!"

"Scuzzy Santas?!" yelled Santa. "All right, buster. That's it!" He lifted his fists and struck a boxing pose. "You asked for it!"

Howard held up his hands, trying for calm. "No, no, no. I'm not going to fight Santa Claus."

"Too bad," said Santa, punching Howard in the jaw, " 'cause Santa's fightin' you!"

Howard exploded. He grabbed the Santa by the front of his costume and threw him into a stack of boxes. A roar of outrage arose from the other Santas.

In the blink of an eye, Santas of all shapes and sizes were piling on Howard Langston. It was all Howard could do just to keep them at bay. Slowly, though, reflexes learned in high school and college flowed back into his muscles. He blocked a high-flying kick from a kung fu Santa, then spun him around and threw him at an onrushing row of assorted Santas. Around the edge of the fight, the Mrs. Clauses started to take bets from the elves and noncombatant Santas. For a brawl, things were developing nicely.

Suddenly the crowd of opponents parted before Howard. From the back of the warehouse came the biggest Santa that Howard had ever seen. This giant replica of the jolly elf shucked his red coat to reveal a massive torso ripped with muscle. He smiled wickedly at Howard and rumbled in a deep bass voice, "I'm gonna deck your halls, bub."

A fist the size of a ham clipped Howard's jaw, knocking him back a few steps. But Howard hadn't been a prize-winning athlete in college for nothing. He recovered quickly and buried his own fist in Giant Santa's gut. As the big elf bent forward from the impact, Howard followed up with an uppercut and a round-house right.

Giant Santa was no slouch in the combat area himself. He rolled with the uppercut and caught Howard's right in a meaty paw. Howard stared in disbelief as his fist was slowly forced backward. "Ho. Ho. Ho," rumbled the Giant Santa.

Howard knew that his only chance lay in ending the fight quickly. As big and strong as Howard might be, the sheer bulk of the Giant Santa would overpower him as soon as his first rush of energy passed. Howard threw caution to the wind—and himself, too! He charged at Giant Santa in an all-out blitz attack.

Caught unprepared by the ferocity of his smaller opponent, Giant Santa soon crumpled and was thrown backward through a stack of toys. He didn't get up again.

Howard smiled grimly but didn't have a chance to savor his victory long. A tidal wave of Santas with an undertow of elves washed over him, bearing him to the concrete floor.

That's when the police smashed the warehouse doors in with battering rams and the trouble *really* started.

6

"It's the Grinch!" yelled the topmost elf of the dog pile that had buried Howard.

Howard didn't know why, but the mountain of bodies on top of him suddenly broke apart and then vanished. When he sat up and saw the massive police raid in progress he realized why everyone had bolted. Then Howard realized that it was probably time for *him* to scoot as well.

"Hey!" snapped an authoritative voice behind Howard. "Who are you?" Howard kept walking, seeking cover among the overstacked aisles. "Buddy—I'm talking to you!"

Howard heard the unsnapping of holsters behind him. His eyes raked the shelves around him for something, anything, that might save him. A box of toy police badges lay on a shelf to his right. Howard snatched one and spun around to face four intense cops.

"This has to be the *sloppiest* bust I have ever seen in my entire career on the force!" Howard barked. The cops took a half step back in surprise.

Howard flashed the toy badge quickly. "Detective Howard Lang. Undercover." He slipped the badge into his coat pocket and walked toward the cops. "I've been working this case for the past three years and you guys come barging in here like a bunch of terrorists at a tea party! The Commissioner's going to hit the roof when he hears about this!"

Howard swaggered slowly past each of the cops, giving them his best mad-dog drill-sergeant impression. "And *look* at you! What kind of men is the academy turning out these days?" He punctuated his inspection with pokes to bellies, arms, and ties. "A bunch of flabby . . . weak . . . sloppy—*disgraces* to the uniform!"

Howard stopped his inspection and stalked toward the door. "I have to get *out* of here! Just the *sight* of you all makes me *sick!*"

Howard only had to flash the badge twice more to get out of the warehouse and to drive out of the parking lot. When he was safely away, driving over a bridge back toward the center of the city, Howard smiled at the toy badge and flipped it out the window. He watched it sail over the guardrail and down toward the water and congratulated himself on his extraordinary luck.

Maybe he should have kept the badge, for at that moment the Suburban's engine began to cough as the car ran out of gas in the middle of the bridge. He had a long time to ponder the fickleness of luck as he slowly pushed his car across the bridge and down the approach, trying to ignore the honking of traffic as it swerved around him.

Jamie and Johnny stood between their houses, feeding handfuls of cereal to Ted's pet reindeer. Several other children and their parents were also gathered around, admiring the animal. One mother walked up to Ted and smiled at him. "You're so considerate," she cooed. "Bringing all this holiday cheer to the neighborhood."

Ted ducked his head humbly. "Christmas comes but once a year."

"You're an amazing man, Ted." The mother sighed. "I wish every husband were more like you." The woman's husband, standing a few yards away, overheard this and glared murderously at Ted. Ted, of course, didn't notice.

A little girl standing near the reindeer asked Johnny, "What's the reindeer's name?"

"I named him Ted," said Johnny proudly. "After my dad."

Jamie looked wistfully at the reindeer. He said to

Johnny, "Your dad is so cool. Wish my dad would do stuff like this."

"He never used to," said Johnny. "Not until he and my mom split up."

Jamie was surprised. "Really?"

Johnny nodded. "Maybe your parents should get a divorce. Did wonders for my dad."

A slow frown slid over Jamie's face, and his brow creased as he pondered this. His shoulders slumped and he shuffled across the yard back toward his house. Liz saw him go and called after him, "Jamie? Sweetie? You okay?"

She got no answer as the small figure disappeared into the house.

The sight of the run-down diner at the foot of the bridge ended Howard's worrying about how bad his morning had been. Instead, he started worrying about how he was going to explain all of this—or *any* of it—to his family.

Howard pushed the Suburban clumsily into a parking slot and stepped into the vestibule of the diner where the pay phone was. He dropped a coin in the slot and waited for the phone to ring. To his surprise, it was answered almost immediately.

"Hello?"

Howard's face automatically broke into a cheery smile. "Jamie! How are you doing, buddy?"

"Dad!" answered Jamie in an excited voice. "Hi! I knew you'd call!"

"Listen, let me talk to Mom."

"You can't."

"Why not?"

"She's next door with Ted."

"She's what?"

"Listen, Dad. Are you on your way? 'Cause the parade's gonna start soon."

"Jamie. Go get your mother, please."

"Well, are you?"

"Am I what?"

"Coming *home* soon."

"Yes. *Immediately*. Now, please get your mother."

" 'Cause, Dad, before you left you *promised* you were gonna be at the parade. And you haven't been here all day, so you *can't* miss it!"

"Jamie, please—"

" 'Cause when someone makes a promise, they definitely should keep it. You know, it's like Turbo Man says, 'Always keep your promises if you wanna keep your friends—' "

"Enough!" shouted Howard, losing patience. "Enough with the Turbo Man, okay! I've had it up to *here* with Turbo Man! If there's anyone I *don't* want advice from right now, it's *Turbo Man!* Now *get your mother!"*

Silence filled the phone line. Howard exhaled deeply

and slowly and tried again. "Aww, Jamie," he said contritely. "I'm sorry. I didn't mean to—"

Jamie's voice sobbed as he answered. "Wh-what would you know about keeping a promise, anyway? You never keep your promises. You never do *anything* you say you're gonna do! *Ever!*"

Click.

That did it. Exhausted, Howard leaned his head against the phone as he hung up the receiver. After a moment, he shuffled over to the counter of the diner and slumped down on a chrome-and-cracked-plastic stool. The waitress took one look and slid a cup of coffee in front of him. "There you go, hon," she said. "Warm you up."

Howard looked at her numbly. "Thanks," he mumbled. He raised the cup up, not drinking yet.

"Cheers," said someone next to Howard, holding out a coffee cup. Howard automatically clinked cups before turning to see who he was toasting with. His eyes widened in shock. "You . . ."

Myron the mailman smiled and sipped his coffee. "Any luck with the doll?"

A dozen answers flashed through Howard's mind, but he rejected them all and settled for a simple "Nah."

"Me, neither," said Myron with a sigh.

Howard sighed as well. As odd as he was, Myron was probably the only person Howard knew who could understand his frustration over the stupid Turbo Man affair. He found himself unburdening his woes. "So I couldn't find the kid a doll. Does that make me a bad father?" He thought for a moment. "No—yelling at him for no good reason. *That* makes me a bad father. . . ."

Myron downed the rest of his cup and motioned for a refill. "It was easier when they were younger," he mused. "Used to be, anything I did for my kid—I was a hero. Now I'm just an old lump." The fresh coffee appeared and Myron sipped carefully. "I work 24-7-365 so he can have everything he wants. But all *he* sees is his old man missin' his ballgames, birthday parties. . . ."

Howard turned to stare at Myron, surprised to hear a version of his own life. Myron plowed on, not noticing. "We get *one day* outta the year to prove we're not total screw-ups and what do we do?" He slammed the coffee cup down, slopping coffee on the counter. "Screw up!"

Howard glanced down and saw his own frowning face staring up at him, reflected in his coffee. "I remember . . . a few years ago. Jamie hadn't even started school yet. I had just quit my job to start my own business. And that Christmas, we barely had enough to pay our bills, so there wasn't much to go around. But I wanted Jamie to have something really special. So I built him his own clubhouse."

Howard smiled at the memory. "The door was a little crooked, and the roof didn't sit straight—but you should've seen his face light up when he saw it. He even made us eat Christmas dinner in it." His smile turned bittersweet, and he leaned back. "*I* was a hero that day."

Howard clapped his hands to his chest. "Now look at me. I'm finally in a place where I can buy him anything he wants, and I can't even come up with one simple toy!" He folded his arms over his belly. "He'll probably never forgive me."

"Yeah, he's gonna need some therapy," agreed Myron. "I know *I* never forgave *my* old man. One Christmas I had my heart set on one of those Johnny 7 OMA guns—one-man army, seven guns in one!—they were the coolest." His coffee was gone already, and he motioned for another refill. "But for my old man, Christmas was just another chance to let me down. I never got a Johnny 7 OMA."

The waitress set the refill in front of Myron, and he downed it in one big gulp. "You ever hear of Henry Starger?" he asked Howard.

"CEO? Starger Industries?"

"My old neighbor. *He* got one." The resentment was clear in Myron's voice. "Now he's a billionaire, and I'm some loser with no future."

For a moment, reality shifted around Howard, and Myron became Jamie, dressed in a shabby postal uniform. Jamie/Myron held up his cup, which Howard knew held something stronger than coffee, and saluted. "Here's to you, Dad," the vision said before dissolving back into just Myron Larrabee.

Terrified, Howard leaped to his feet. "I can't let this happen! It's just a doll! A stupid little plastic doll! There's gotta be one out there somewhere!"

"You say you're looking for a Turbo Man doll?" crackled a new voice in the diner. Howard looked around in confusion. "You say you'd do anything to get your hands on one?"

"Yes! Yes! Yes!" cried Howard, sure that he'd gone completely over the edge but not caring anymore.

"Well, WKRS has *good news* for *you!"* The radio! Howard and Myron turned to stare at the little plastic box above the grill. "If you're the first caller who can name all *seven* of Santa's reindeer, you'll be the winner of your very own Turbo Man doll. Just call 555-WKRS—now!"

Howard and Myron bolted from their stools toward the pay phone at the same time. They reached the phone in a dead heat and began to struggle for possession of the receiver. Howard caught Myron with a hip shot that tumbled the mailman into the front booth of the diner. While Myron thrashed in the booth, Howard had time to drop a coin in and dial.

Then Myron threw himself at Howard's back and started choking him with both hands. Howard beat Myron on the head with the receiver until the mailman's hands slipped loose. He got the receiver back to his ear in time to hear it pick up at the radio station. "Hello, WKRS!"

"Yes!" shouted Howard. "I know it! It's—"

With a jerk and a snap, Myron yanked the receiver cord out of the pay phone. Howard shoved the disconnected phone into Myron's chest, knocking the heavy man backward. "What are you doing? I got through!"

Before the situation could become a barroom brawl, the waitress called out to the struggling men, "Hey, fellas! That radio station's just a few blocks from here!"

Howard and Myron paused. The radio voice crackled again. "Looks like I'll have to take another caller. Remember, that's 555-WKRS! You could be the proud owner of the hottest toy since the Johnny 7 OMA!"

Myron got a millisecond's lead on Howard. He grabbed a wreath that hung over the diner's doorway, jammed it down over Howard's head and eyes, and sprinted outside.

Howard tore the wreath to shreds and dashed out after Myron. Even though Myron had a good half-block lead on him, Howard was in much better shape and so quickly caught up with the mailman. The radio station came into view at the end of the street, and Howard pumped on past Myron, breathlessly chanting, "Dasher. Dancer. Prancer. Vixen. Comet. Cupid. Donner. Blitzen . . ."

WKRS Radio occupied the tenth floor of a steel-and-glass building at the dead end of the street. As Howard entered the lobby, he could hear the on-air broadcast being piped down to the lobby. A caller was reciting,

"Uh . . . Randy, Jermaine, Tito . . ." The deejay cut the caller off as Howard repeatedly stabbed the Up button on the elevator. "Nope. Sorry. Next caller."

The audio was also piped into the elevator. As Howard rode up impatiently, he heard, "Ah . . . Lancer, Flasher, Nixon . . ." The line went dead. "Sorry. *Next* caller." The deejay snickered.

The elevator stopped and Howard raced across the station lobby to the plate-glass window fronting the broadcast booth. He pounded on the window to get the deejay's attention. "Let me in!" Howard shouted. "I know the answer!"

The deejay's eyes popped open at the sight of the large frantic man at his window. He picked up the phone and dialed 911.

Thinking that the deejay was taking another caller, Howard slammed his shoulder into the booth door. The door burst inward, tumbling Howard with it. The deejay dropped the phone and cowered in the farthest corner of the booth. Howard got up from the floor and shouted in the poor man's face, "Dasher, Dancer, Prancer, Vixen, Comet, Cupid, Donner, and Blitzen!"

The deejay cowered in absolute terror. Howard tried to explain. "I couldn't get through on the phone. Do I win?"

The deejay didn't get a chance to answer. Myron Larrabee burst into the booth. Howard turned and snarled, "Too late! I had the right answer!"

Myron's face was lit with an irrational glow. He held

up a small square box wrapped in plain brown paper. "I don't need the right answer to win." He smiled maniacally.

"What's that," asked Howard, staring at the box.

"That, my friend, is a homemade explosive device."

"A *bomb?"*

"In layman's terms, yes. A bomb."

Howard gawked. "You *built* a bomb?"

"Nah." Myron shrugged. "Hundreds of these li'l buggers come through the post office every year. I lifted one. Figured it might come in handy one day." He glared at the deejay. "Now gimme the doll or I'll blow this place sky-high."

Howard spoke soothingly, trying to defuse the situation. "Myron. Come on, buddy. Just give me the package." He held out a hand. "It's Christmas. I'm sure we can work something out—"

Myron's eyes blazed. *"Buddy?!* I'm not your buddy! You're the last person I wanna work anything out with! This all *started* with you!" He waggled the package at Howard. "I offered to team up! But *noooo*—you had other plans for Myron Larrabee, didn't you? Leaving me alone in that toy store, fending off thousands of rabid shoppers! Plain common civilians! *Letter writers!* The same people who persecute me for wearing my knee socks in the summer—and who make fun of my safari hat!"

Howard and the deejay looked at each other in amazement. Myron, meanwhile, was caught up in his recitation of injuries. "And put their trash cans in front of their mailboxes so I have to get outta my Jeep! I mean, the door's on that side for a *reason!* And then they expect me to just—*deliver their mail*—like I have no feelings of my *own?"* Myron's rage overflowed into a fit of trembling that jolted the box from his hand. It plummeted toward the floor.

"Hit the dirt!" yelled Howard.

7

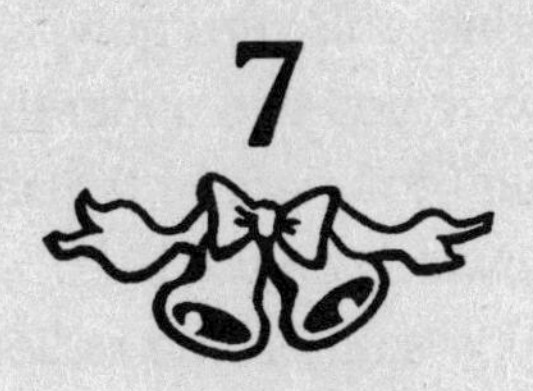

The deejay dived behind his desk. Howard simply dropped. The package seemed to tumble in slow motion toward the floor, spinning lazily on its way down. It hit the carpet and bounced once.

Then a music-box version of "Jingle Bells" started plinking from inside.

Howard crawled over to the box and ripped it open. Inside, a cheap metal music box continued to play the Christmas tune. He glared at Myron. "*This* is the bomb?" he roared, throwing the box down.

Myron flashed a sheepish grin just before Howard launched himself at the mailman and pinned him to the wall. "You twisted little worm," he snarled, drawing his fist back to launch a haymaker.

"Excuse me. Gentlemen?" the deejay interrupted, peering up over his desk.

Howard and Myron both looked over at the deejay.

"I hate to bring this up now," the deejay said hesitantly, "but were you two under the impression that I had a Turbo Man doll here in the studio?"

"Yes," said Howard, puzzled.

"That's what you said on the radio," Myron added.

The deejay grimaced and nervously flexed his fingers. "Uh, actually, no. I said whoever won would *get* a doll. *Eventually.*" He picked up a slip of paper and waved it. "All we have here is a gift certificate."

"A *gift certificate?*" shouted Howard and Myron in unison.

The deejay had his confidence back. "Sure. You can pick up a doll at the store," he said breezily. "Soon as they get more in stock."

Howard had his hands around the deejay's throat before he heard the approaching sirens. He glanced around in alarm. "Did you call the cops?" The deejay might have tried to answer, but Howard's hands kept his head from moving.

Myron bolted out of the booth, knocking over a stack of cartridges. Howard let go of the deejay and started to follow, but he slipped on the fallen tapes and crashed to the floor. Myron made it to the elevator and punched the button, calling back to Howard, "Better luck next time, loser!"

Myron's cackle was cut short when the elevator doors opened and he faced a dozen policemen, their guns all drawn and pointed right at him. "You wouldn't shoot a fellow civil servant, would you, fellas?" he squeaked.

In answer, the cops cocked their guns.

Howard neatly avoided the confrontation at the elevator by heading for the stairwell door. He yanked it open and was greeted by the sight of Officer Hummell, his gun drawn, leading a backup squad up the stairwell. The look of shock on Hummell's face was replaced by a slow wry smile. "You just can't stay out of trouble," he said, recognizing Howard.

Howard backed out into the hallway, joining Myron, who was retreating from the cops in the elevator. Myron suddenly whipped a small square package from his mail sack and held it up menacingly. "I am holding a homemade explosive device!" he shouted. "Drop your guns or I blow this place sky-high!"

Howard was dumbfounded. But when Hummell and the other cops slowly lowered their weapons, Howard sidled past them into the stairwell exit. Officer Hummell glared at him but was helpless in the face of Myron's threat.

Myron, meanwhile, ordered the cops out of the elevator and took their place. Gently, he set the box down on the floor as the elevator doors closed.

With both suspects gone, the cops all stood frozen, staring at the ominous package on the floor. Hummell broke the spell. He walked up to the box and very, very gently picked it up. From arm's length, he inspected it.

"You shouldn't mess with that," a young cop quavered.

Hummell shot him a scornful look. "Relax, Sparky. I spent ten years on the bomb squad." He resumed his inspection of the box, sniffing it, shaking it gently and holding it to his ear.

"Gentlemen, we've been duped," Hummell said, relaxing. "This is nothing but a harmless Christmas package." He picked at the wrapping.

Howard was already at the corner of the building when Myron came racing out the front door. An instant later, a brilliant flash of light and a loud explosion burst from the tenth floor. Howard saw Myron stop and gape up at the radio station. "Shoot," he heard the mailman say. "I thought that was a fruitcake!" And with that, Myron raced away.

On the tenth floor, the smoke slowly cleared to reveal a crowd of cops, as sooty as coal miners, but otherwise unharmed. The young cop wiped his face, which only served to smear the dirt around, and pinned Hummell with a dark look. "How many years on the bomb squad?" he asked dryly.

Howard sat next to the burly driver of the tow truck and thought about what to do next. He was in a tow truck because by the time he had made it back to his car at the diner, he had found his faithful green Suburban stripped. Completely. Even the doors had been stolen.

As the tow truck was bringing his hapless car back home, Howard was trying out various apology speeches on the driver. "Liz, honey, I did everything within my power to get that doll for Jamie. But look! I got a gift certificate! Which is just as good!"

"Too cheery," critiqued the driver. "Gotta be stronger."

Howard tried a sterner tone. "Look, Liz. I ran around all day like a crazy person looking for that stupid doll. And if Jamie's upset—well, that's just too bad!"

"Heartless," said the driver. "Show a little emotion."

Howard tried again. "Oh, Liz. I'm so sorry. I didn't get one. I failed as a husband. I failed as a father. Can you ever forgive me?"

The driver looked over at Howard with a disgusted look. "Whyn't ya just put on a dress an' weep like a little girl?" he sneered.

"Forget it." Howard sighed, slumping in the passenger seat as the truck neared his house. "I'm sunk."

Inside the Langston home, Ted stood on a stepladder, holding a decorative star ornament inches above the top of the Langston Christmas tree. He looked down at Liz with friendly disapproval.

"Sorry about that, Ted," Liz said. "But that's Howard's job. He *always* puts the star on. He's adamant about that."

Ted shrugged and climbed down the ladder, handing the star to Liz when he was done. "Too bad he's not as adamant about spending time with his family on Christmas Eve."

Liz turned on Ted, ready to defend Howard. But then she realized that she really couldn't, so she frowned and turned away.

The tow truck dropped Howard off in front of his house and then trundled the wrecked Suburban off to the body shop. Howard started trudging up his driveway when he looked through his living-room window—Ted Maltin was holding the Christmas star! Howard shook with outrage. "That son of a—! I'm out all day and he's inside putting up *my* star!" Howard started forward. "On *my* tree!"

And then he stopped. A rapid chain of thoughts flashed through Howard's brain. Ted. Christmas tree. Present. Turbo Man. *"I got a Turbo Man for Johnny months ago. It's nestled safely under our tree . . ."* Howard stood on the driveway and looked over at the Maltin house next door.

Ted was divorced and had Johnny only on weekends and split holidays. That meant that no one was home right now in the Maltin house. A sly grin crept over Howard's face as he looked back at his own living room. "I'll show him," he muttered.

Minutes later, Howard was jimmying the front door of Ted's house with a plastic card. In seconds, the door opened and Howard slipped inside. The living room of the Maltin house was typically Ted—everything overdone. A nearly life-size Nativity scene was arranged around the flickering fireplace, complete with fiberglass Wise Men, shepherds, and sheep gathered around a manger filled with real straw. The Christmas tree would have reached the ceiling if its branches didn't droop under the weight of every imaginable ornament.

Howard tiptoed over to the tree. Even the present for Johnny was typically Ted—wrapped in Turbo Man paper, there was no surprise to its contents. Howard picked it up and shook it. From inside, slightly muffled, he heard, "It's Turbo Time!" Howard smiled and tucked the box under his arm and headed back to the front door.

As his hand touched the knob, Howard heard singing outside. He peeped through the curtains of the front windows and saw a group of carolers standing on Ted's front lawn. Worse yet, he could see his wife, Liz, with Ted right next to her, standing on the stoop of the Langston house, listening to the carolers.

Thwarted, Howard's eyes raked the inside of Ted's house. "The back door!" he said, remembering. He moved quickly through the house and out the back door. Once out in the backyard, he paused to ponder the best way to make it into his own yard.

A glint of light reflected off the shiny present in Howard's hands and made him look at it carefully for the first time. Taped to the top of the box was a small gift tag that read, "To Johnny. Love, Dad."

Reality caught up with Howard for the first time that day. "What am I doing?" he said. "Look at me—

stealing from a kid. I can't do this! Enough, Howard. You lost. Face it like a man."

Howard had resolved to put the present back under Ted's tree when a snuffling sound made him look up—directly into the eyes of Ted's reindeer. The big animal snorted and pawed the ground, gathering himself for a charge. "Down boy," soothed Howard. "It's okay . . ." But the reindeer wasn't buying it. He dropped his head and rushed at Howard.

Howard broke and ran for the back door as fast as he could. Being in a hurry, he neglected to close the door behind him, so the reindeer followed him right into the house!

With the reindeer hard on his heels, Howard sprinted into the kitchen and swung on into the living room. He slipped on the polished wood floor and plowed into the Nativity scene. The head of a Wise Man flew off his shoulders and into the fireplace. There was no time for Howard to rescue it; he had to scramble to his feet and outrun the reindeer.

Howard led the angry beast down the hallway where he spotted the open door to Ted's home office. He ran into the office, ducking behind the door. When the reindeer barged into the office, Howard shot out from behind the door into the hallway, this time remembering to close the door.

As he leaned against the door to catch his breath, he could hear and feel the reindeer butting the door with its antlers. Luckily, he had kept his hold on the wrapped Turbo Man. It was time to put it back under the tree.

He took one step toward the living room and nearly had a heart attack when a shrill electronic ringing screamed through the house. Howard looked up to see the smoke alarm flashing. There was a fire somewhere!

The living room. Howard ran in to find the Wise Man's head burning merrily in the fireplace, belching noxious clouds of sooty smoke into the air and panicking the smoke alarm. Howard grabbed the poker from its rack and hooked the burning head out of the fireplace and onto the carpet, which cheerfully began to burn as well. With the alarm yammering in his ears and the head threatening to burn the whole house down, Howard did the only thing he could think of—he kicked the head out the front window.

Accompanied by the sound of shattering glass, the flaming bearded head landed at the feet of the carolers, who immediately screamed and scattered. Ted saw the head and shrieked, "Someone's in my house!" Followed by Liz, he raced back to his home.

Howard had stomped out the carpet fire and was now trying to silence the smoke alarm. It was mounted too high for him to reach it and pull the battery, so he simply knocked it off the wall with the poker. Without missing a beat, he followed through by leaping over the sofa toward the tree. He bent down to replace the Turbo Man.

"Howard?" came Liz's voice from the door.

Howard stood up, still holding the package. Through the broken window, he could see Liz and Ted crossing the lawn. Howard tried to look nonchalant. "Oh. Hi," he said.

Ted noticed the burning Wise Man's head. "Balthazar!" he yelped, running to the head and smothering the flames with his sweater.

Liz just looked at Howard. "What are you doing?" she demanded.

Howard gaped. "Uh, I—"

Liz noticed the present in Howard's hands. "What is that?"

Ted looked up from his grieving over Balthazar. "That's Johnny's Turbo Man!" he cried in outrage.

"What?" said Liz.

"Wait! It's not what you think—" began Howard.

"Oh, it isn't?" said Liz scornfully. "Really! Then do tell me what it *is!* Because as far as *I* know, you got Jamie his *own* Turbo Man weeks ago!" When Howard couldn't meet her eyes, she continued. "Howard, I've seen you do some pretty thoughtless things. But . . . breaking into our neighbor's house and stealing presents from under his tree?"

"Liz," said Howard. "If you'd just give me a second—"

"I sat home all day explaining to our son why his father wasn't home yet, and I wasn't even close! Was I?"

"Okay. Look. I know parts of this are going to sound completely ridiculous, but please . . . let me tell you the truth."

"I don't think so, Howard. I've been listening to your version of the truth for far too long now, and honestly, I don't want to hear any more. All I want to do is salvage what's left of Christmas Eve. And go to the parade with my son."

Howard crumpled. "Okay. I understand. Let's go."

"No."

"What?" said Howard in disbelief.

Liz took a deep breath. "I think it'd be better for everyone if you just stayed home." She turned away. "You've already done enough damage." She started walking back to her house.

"Liz! Wait—"

But she ignored him and called to Ted, "Ted, would you drive us?"

Ted nodded to Liz, then looked back in confusion at Howard. "Honestly, Howard," he said sadly. "And on Christmas Eve." He turned to follow Liz.

Howard stood thunderstruck in the doorway of Ted's house. He felt numb. He felt like he couldn't move. Then, with a splintering crash, the reindeer burst through the office door and charged directly at Howard.

The sun was low in the sky as Howard sat on his own back porch, nursing a soft drink. He leaned against the clubhouse he had built for Jamie, perversely enjoying the pain of the rough wood digging into his back. He stared moodily at the reindeer next to him, agreeably drinking soda out of a cereal bowl. Somehow a truce had been called between them, and it had slipped into an odd friendship. "Looks like it's just you and me this evening, huh, Rudolph?"

The reindeer continued to slurp up its drink, pausing only to emit a thunderous belch. Howard's gaze slid from the animal to the clubhouse. His eyes filled with tears as he remembered the warm family feeling he'd had when he had given it to Jamie. Inside the clubhouse, he could see that Jamie had decorated the walls with pinned-up drawings. The one he could see clearest was a crude rendering of a boat next to a palm-tree-covered island, both surrounded by wavy blue lines to indicate an ocean. Three figures stood on the boat, two tall and one small. Carefully labeled despite childishly scrawled letters, the figures were labeled "Mom," "Dad," and "Me." The "Dad" and "Me" figures were holding hands.

A wave of sadness washed over Howard. He crushed the aluminum can in his hand and stood up with an air of resolve. Finished with its drink, the reindeer nuzzled Howard's crumpled can. "Sorry, buddy. You're on your own." He tossed the can in the trash. "It's time I started keeping my promises." He strode purposefully out of the yard. The reindeer belched and watched him go.

8

Downtown was a huge, grand Christmas celebration. The main street, festooned with wreaths and countless holiday decorations, was crowded with families bundled against the cold, sipping hot chocolate, and strolling their way past lines of vendors hawking seasonal souvenirs.

A large banner stretched high across the width of the street, proclaiming in glittering letters, Twelfth Holiday Wintertainment Parade! To one side, a wobbly platform rose almost as high as the banner—the parade reviewing stand, overflowing with cameras and broadcast equipment, and captained by the biggest stars of local TV.

The two female TV personalities, Liza and Gale, took their duties as commentators very seriously. Nearly interchangeable, with similar capped teeth, big hair, and heavy makeup, they smiled as hard as they could and huddled close to the microphones that carried their comments to the PA system strung up along the street.

"Looks like it's that time of year again—the twelfth annual Holiday Wintertainment Parade," the first woman addressed the camera lens. "I'm weatherperson Gale Force, here with Liza Tisch, of *AM Live.*"

Liza hugged her partner. "Merry Christmas, Gale!" she chirped, then turned back to the camera. "We're high atop Channel Five's Parade Central to keep *you* updated on all of this year's parade action!"

Below them, the Santa Marching Band strutted into action, blasting out a brassy version of "Joy to the World," to the enthusiastic cheers of the spectators. Behind them appeared a float in the shape of a huge snow dome. As it joggled down the street, giant snowflakes swirled inside the glass dome, spinning in the wake of a Frosty the Snowman as he skated on a ring of ice. It looked like the perfect suburban dream of Christmas.

Ted Maltin's car had stopped as close to the police barricades as possible. Inside, the kids in the backseat were clamoring to be set free to enjoy the celebration. "The parade's already started!" cried Jamie.

"Hey, Dad!" shouted Johnny, pointing out the window. "There's Owen and his dad! Can we go stand with them? While you park the car? Please?"

Ted looked at Liz Langston, sitting in the front seat

next to him. Liz looked at her son and then nodded to Ted. Ted turned back to the boys and smiled. "Okay. We'll meet you there."

As the boys scrambled out of the car, Liz called after them, "Don't go wandering off!" They ran to join their friend Owen, and then all three boys wormed their way through the crowd to claim front-row seats on the curb.

"Check it out!" said Jamie, already impressed. An array of life-size toys danced and marched in place right in front of them. Raggedy Ann and Andy waltzed circles around a strutting Mister Machine. A row of Nutcracker soldiers skirmished with a troop of G.I. Joes. There were Monopoly game pieces, Cabbage Patch kids, even a monster-size Etch-A-Sketch. In a pink Corvette rode Ken and Barbie.

"You see Turbo Man?" said Johnny, craning to see the far end of the parade.

Jamie shook his head. "They're saving him for last." Johnny gave up looking and both boys became absorbed in the parade.

Back in the car, Liz stared out the window in sadness and disappointment, Howard's absence weighing her down like an anchor. Next to her, Ted fished a personalized Thermos from under the seat. Labeled Ted's Eggnog, he uncapped it and turned to Liz. "Oh, Liz," he said sympathetically. "I'm sorry you had to go through that back there." He poured the drink into the cup. "Here. Have some nonalcoholic eggnog."

Liz smiled wanly and waved the cup away. "I'll be fine."

Ted leaned closer. "You can't hide your feelings from me," he said earnestly. "Go on. Let it out. Get it out of your system." He offered the cup again.

Liz pushed the cup away this time. "No. Really, Ted. I'm okay."

"I don't think so, Liz," said Ted, staring deeply into her eyes. "You're like a lost and frightened foal. I can see it in your eyes. Don't worry . . . Ted's here."

Liz drew away, pressing back against the door. "Thanks," she said nervously. "You're very sweet . . ."

"You deserve better, Lizzie."

"Lizzie?"

"Someone you can talk to. A shoulder to cry on." Liz slid her hand behind her, trying to find the door handle. Ted continued, "It's useless, Liz. We can't hide our feelings for each other any longer."

"Feelings?"

"I don't need to tell you, Liz. I'm a *very* eligible bachelor. There are lots of women who would give anything to be in your position right now."

Liz was appalled but tried to maintain her composure. "I'm sure of that—"

"But I've chosen you."

Liz grinned a sickly smile. "I'm a lucky, lucky girl."

Ted suddenly leaned forward. "Enough talking." He puckered his lips.

* * *

Many blocks away, on the other side of the parade, Howard fumed in the backseat of a taxi that sat glued in the middle of a horrible traffic jam. "Can't you take Fourth Avenue?" he complained to the driver.

The driver, who got paid as long as the meter was running, was unperturbed by the delay. "Sorry, pal," he drawled. "All the roads are packed. *Everybody's* trying to get to the parade."

Howard seethed with impatience. He checked his watch for the tenth time in five minutes and gritted his teeth. Suddenly he pulled some bills out of his pocket, threw them at the driver, and climbed out of the cab.

Out on the street, Howard ran quickly, dodging between cars as motionless as his taxi had been. When he reached the sidewalk, he stopped to get his bearings. On the horizon, the skyline of the town had something moving across it—a round wobbling object. Howard shaded his eyes with his hand and the round thing came into focus. It was the giant Santa face balloon, a perennial favorite of the parade. Howard was close to his goal. He ran down the sidewalk and soon settled into an easy, distance-eating lope.

Within minutes, Howard had reached the concession stands that formed a wall along the parade route. Scouring the far side of the street for a glimpse of Liz and Jamie, he spotted Ted's car parked in the public lot. Even though the windows were a little fogged up, Howard could recognize his wife and his neighbor inside the car—and Ted was leaning forward to kiss Liz!

Heedless of anything else, Howard raced toward the car.

In the car, Liz reacted with unthinking quickness. She snatched up the Thermos and threw it at Ted's face. He jerked back in his seat and dumped the cup of eggnog all over himself. While he gasped for breath, Liz finally found the door handle, yanked it open, and leaped out of the car, rapidly disappearing into the parade-watching crowd.

Ted slowly wiped the eggnog from his eyes and slumped back into his seat. "Well," he muttered, "*that* didn't exactly go as well as I had hoped."

In his rush toward Ted's car, Howard paid little attention to the foot traffic around him. When he collided with a man carrying a tray of drinks and snacks, it came as a surprise to both of them.

Splat! A cup of hot chocolate fell off the man's tray. "Hey, buddy," barked the victim, "watch where you're—" Howard locked eyes with the man. It was Officer Hummell. The cop's eyes widened with rage as he recognized Howard. "You—"

All thought of Ted and Liz vanished from Howard's mind. He turned and bolted toward an alley. Officer Hummell tried to shift the tray of drinks to one hand so he could draw his gun. He shouted after Howard, "Stop! Get back here!" The drinks went sailing through the air, and Hummell took off after Howard.

Meanwhile, Howard's escape route took him into the parade staging area. Desperately, he dodged workers and costumed characters, and tried not to get run down by floats being maneuvered into position. The good thing about his route was that he soon left the furious Officer Hummell behind. The bad thing about it was that, in all the festive confusion, Howard had no idea where he was going.

That was how he suddenly found himself facing a brick wall in a dead-end alley between two warehouses. Doors into the warehouses opened to his left and his right. Howard could almost feel Hummell catching up, so he picked a door at random and walked inside that warehouse.

When his eyes adjusted to the darkness, Howard saw that he was surrounded by dozens of cops, all putting the finishing touches on the police department float. The float, in the shape of a huge papier-mâché policeman, loomed over Howard. "Oops!" he muttered, and quickly backed outside again.

He ran across the alley into the other warehouse, sure that whatever it contained had to be safer than trying to hide from a cop by standing in the middle of an army of cops. He slipped past the door just in time—from inside the darkness, Howard saw Officer Hummell push his way through the crowds of workers and come to a confused stop when he saw the dead end.

Howard ducked behind the warehouse door to avoid

Hummell. Suddenly a voice behind him shouted, "You!"

Howard turned to see a parade worker approaching him. "Yeah?" he said nervously.

"Who are you?" snapped the worker. "Are you the guy?"

Howard risked a look out the door. Hummell was still standing outside, looking around for his fugitive. "Mmm . . . yeah," said Howard, bluffing. "Sure. I'm the guy."

"Thank heaven," said the worker in obvious relief. He grabbed Howard by the arm and hustled him farther into the warehouse, talking quickly as they went. "Okay, we're running late here, so pay attention." A team of float workers converged on Howard, fitting him into some elaborate costume. The boss worker continued to lecture him, ticking off items on a clipboard. "You already read the manual we sent you so you know all about the important controls. Let me just go over a few of the changes. There are *three* cutoff valves for the nitro fluid—here, here, and here. The normal readout on the pressure gauge should read anywhere below fifty. *Not seventy,* like you were told earlier!"

Howard tried to get a word in edgewise, but the boss only spoke faster. "Your emergency cutoff switch is here," he said, tapping the chest plate of the costume that was being strapped to Howard's torso. "There's also a microphone in the helmet that will alter your voice to the proper range and tonality. The procedure is the same as we talked about on the phone. Stick to that and there won't be any trouble."

"Look," began Howard. "I don't think—"

The boss worker clapped Howard on the back and smiled at him. "Before you say anything," he interrupted, "let *me* speak for everyone when I thank you for filling in for Pete on such short notice. It was a *total* freak accident at the rehearsal, and we're confident that we've got *all* the kinks worked out of the system."

"Accident?" Howard gulped. "What—" He was cut off as two workers behind him lowered a helmet on his head and snugged it into the costume's collar.

The boss looked up from his clipboard into Howard's eyes. "Oh, and you should know"—he flashed a quick smile of reassurance—"the doctors said Pete actually showed some brain activity this morning. That's a *really* good sign!" He gave Howard an earnest thumbs-up.

Howard's protests were drowned out as the rest of the crew gave him a round of applause. A minute later, he was hustled bodily under the open skirt of an elaborate float. Darkness swallowed him.

When his eyes adjusted, Howard could barely see the man in the pink fuzzy costume who took charge of him under the float. He had the smell of a chain-smoker and the disposition of a cab driver who'd never gotten a tip. He hustled Howard through a door in the base of the float and into a small tubelike compartment. "Where the heck have you been?" the smoky man groused. "I been sweatin' like a dog in here, waitin' for you to show up!"

The float began to move out of the warehouse, joggling Howard off balance. Enough light seeped in to let him see his companion better. "It's show time," announced his partner, putting on the oversize head of the costume.

Howard's jaw dropped as he recognized the costume. "You . . . that's . . ." The floor beneath the two men began to rise—they were standing on a hydraulic lift. "You're *Booster!"* Howard gawked.

They were moving up through a hole in the float. "Booster" swung his big pink head toward Howard, and his voice came from inside, only slightly muffled by the foot-long tusks that dropped from the saber-toothed tiger's jaws. "Yeah, and who d'ya think *you* are? Mary Poppins?"

Daylight filled the shaft as the float moved out into the street. Howard looked down at himself for the first time and recognized the red-and-gold costume that he was wearing. "Oh, my . . ." He couldn't believe it. "I'm *Turbo Man!"*

9

Jamie and Johnny sat on the curb, fidgeting with impatience. They had long since gotten tired of dancing toys and pretty girls riding in the local auto dealers' best cars. There was only one thing they wanted to see.

Then Liza Tisch's perky voice crackled out of the PA system. "And now, the moment you've all been waiting for!" A triple-decker float turned the far corner of the parade route and headed for the reviewing stand. "Here he is, boys and girls—live and in person! TURBO MAN!"

The crowd cheered as the float lumbered forward. Then every kid whooped and yelled, and parents clapped heartily as the hydraulic lift brought the costumed Howard and his fuzzy pink sidekick to the top of the float.

Howard stood frozen in panic, staring at all the

cheering people lining the street. Booster nudged Howard with an elbow. "Wave, you idiot! Wave!"

Howard waved at the crowd. The audience responded by doubling their volume. Flashbulbs popped, kids squealed, and grown men raised their fists in happy salute. The intense wave of emotion made Howard tingle. The projected good feelings warmed him, loosened him up, and he started waving in earnest. He spread his legs in a superhero pose and threw out his chest. Now he wanted to look the part.

Down the street, Jamie and Johnny jumped up and down as the float approached. Liz made it through the crowd to stand next to her son. She clapped her hands and added her whistles to the excited clamor.

Howard's entire world shifted gear. All the manic frustration of the day drained away as he soaked up the adulation of his adoring fans. He *was* Turbo Man now. People cheered and squealed when he waved directly at them. Overhead, an announcement from the viewing stand added to the frenzy. "Liza," Gale's voice bubbled, "in a few moments, Turbo Man himself will select a special child from the audience!"

Not to be outperked, Liza smiled harder and added in her cheeriest voice, "And that child will be the lucky winner of a *special edition* Turbo Man doll!"

Booster reached into a hidden compartment on the float and took out a Turbo Man doll and displayed it to the crowds. The winter sunlight reflected off the gleaming doll, whose golden parts were plated with genuine gold. The pink saber-toothed tiger waited until Howard's cycle of waving brought him around to face his sidekick again. "Here," Booster said, thrusting the doll at Howard. *"You're* supposed to be holding this!"

Howard almost choked. There it was, the object of all his trials today, the prize he'd been fighting for so hard. He gulped but couldn't move.

"Hello?" yelled Booster. "Wake up! You're missing all your cues!"

Howard took the doll, staring at it in awe. Then he raised it up over his head to the deafening cheers of the crowd. Howard blew them kisses.

Booster watched Howard's grandstanding with wonder and scorn. He leaned over and stage-whispered into his ear, "Hey, Rock Star! Better stay on your toes. Dementor's jumping the float in a couple of blocks." He waved in the general direction of a tall building up ahead.

The building was crowned with a gigantic metal Christmas tree, the town's central display. Hundreds of lights and ornaments sparkled and shone. At the base of the tree, out of sight from spectators below, a steel rig anchored a cable that ran from the roof downward to the street. A young stuntman in a Dementor costume checked the rigging and looked at his watch. It was almost time. He hefted the costume's helmet, but before he could don it, a shadowy figure hit him in the head with one of the oversize ornaments from the tree.

The stuntman fell limply to the roof. The attacker dragged the body into the shadows . . .

Booster, meanwhile, was losing patience with his clueless partner. He interrupted Howard's mugging with a growled, "Pick a kid already, will you?" Howard gave him a blank look. Booster twitched. "Jeez! Do I have to walk you through this whole gig? Pick a kid." His arm swept across the crowd. "From the audience. To come up here and get his prize." He pointed at the doll.

"Oh," said Howard, finally catching on.

Jamie and Johnny were hopping up and down with excitement. The Turbo Man float had stopped in front of them and it looked like the special-edition prize was going to be given out! "Pick me! Pick me! Pick *me!*" they screamed, trying to outscream hundreds of other kids.

Turbo Man walked to the edge of the float near their side of the street. The unseen eyes behind the visor raked the crowd, stopping at the two boys standing side by side. "He's looking at *me!*" cried Jamie in surprise.

His friend wouldn't even think of it. "Naw! He's lookin' at me!" Johnny insisted.

Turbo Man raised his arm and pointed directly at the two boys. Jamie and Johnny immediately began to argue. "See that," cheered Jamie. "He's pointing at *me!*"

"Naw! It's me!"

"Me!"

"Meee!"

The booming, electronically deepened voice of Turbo Man rang out as he continued to point. "Jamie!"

Johnny stared at his friend. Liz positively gawked at her son. "He knows my name?" said Jamie, more stunned than they were.

Turbo Man beckoned to Jamie, urging the boy to climb up on the float. Jamie stood in place, paralyzed.

"Well, Liza," chirped Gale over the PA system, "it looks like Turbo Man has selected a *winner!"*

Liz kissed the still-stunned boy on the cheek. His best friend nudged him in the ribs. "Go on," Johnny said with a tight smile. "If you don't, *I* will!"

Jamie ran out into the street and clambered up onto the Turbo Man float. He walked up the stairs until he stood directly in front of his hero. He swallowed nervously, trembling with excitement. Turbo Man, by now a blur of red and gold to Jamie, held out the special-edition doll and said, "Merry Christmas, Jamie."

Jamie was thrilled beyond belief. In a small voice, he stammered, "H-h-how did you know my name?"

Turbo Man smiled and said, "Because, Jamie. It's *me.* Your—"

Turbo Man didn't get to finish. A shadow swooped down onto the float, landing with a thump on the top tier. Liza, acting on her cue, shouted, "Oh, no, kids! It's

Turbo Man's archenemy, Dementor!" The crowd booed the villain loudly. He, in turn, shot a rude gesture back at them. Gale covered her microphone, confused. Shifting papers around, she asked Liza, "Was that in the script?"

Dementor wasn't following the script, but he was acting in character. He grabbed Jamie and yanked him close. "Okay, kid," he growled. "Gimme the doll and nobody gets hurt!"

Turbo Man stared at Dementor and gasped. "Myron?"

10

Howard's brain spun from absolute joy to utter confusion at the sound of the mailman's voice coming from Dementor. The villain lifted his helmet and left no doubt. It was impossible, but it was Myron, all right!

"That's right, smart guy! Thought you could outsmart me again, huh? Pretty slick with that *costume* idea. But I'm one step ahead of you. As usual!" Mad lights danced in Myron's eyes.

Howard tried to be reasonable. "Myron, come on—you're taking this *too* far!"

Myron reddened. He flared his nostrils and gnashed his teeth. "I'm not going home without that doll!" he insisted. He snapped his helmet back down.

Booster ambled over and tapped Dementor on the back. "Hey, buddy," he complained. "This ain't how we rehearsed it—"

Myron spun and punched Booster smack in the middle of his furry pink face. The saber-toothed tiger fell down the slopes of the float and tumbled into the street. Immediately, a horde of kids ducked under and around the barricades to pummel the sidekick. The rest of the crowd booed enthusiastically.

Back on the float, Jamie took advantage of the confusion to stuff the Turbo Man doll into his backpack. Then he scrambled down the float toward the lowest tier. Myron caught Jamie before the boy could jump off, grabbing him and clutching him close.

Jamie struggled wildly in Myron's arms. He couldn't break free, but he landed a few good punches, one of which hit a button on the Dementor suit. Suddenly dense smoke erupted from the suit, surrounding them both. The arms around Jamie slackened their grip, and the boy ran out of the cloud toward the far side of the float. "You'll never get away with this, Dementor!" Jamie shouted.

Myron was coughing and flapping his arms to disperse the smoke. "C'mon, kid," he said angrily. "Don't be a pain in the rump!" He lunged at Jamie.

Howard's blood was boiling. He ran down the stairway of the float toward Myron and Jamie. "Hey! Get away from him!"

The entire float shook as Howard ran. That got Myron's attention away from Jamie for the moment. He looked up to see Howard running at him. Myron raised a fist at Howard and twisted it. With a loud *sproinng,* the arm-extension mechanism propelled his steel fist forward. It hit Howard hard, knocking him off his feet.

Up on the reviewing stand, Liza and Gale had abandoned their scripts and begun ad-libbing comments like sportscasters. "Uh-oh, Liza!" Gale frowned. "It looks like Dementor's beaten Turbo Man!"

"Oh, no, Gale," Liza chimed in sadly. "This could be the end of civilization as we know it!"

The crowd on the street wouldn't stand for this. Loud voices shouted out, "Come on, Turbo Man! Stop Dementor! Save the kid! You can do it!" More voices joined in.

Myron was doggedly trying to rip open Jamie's backpack. Jamie struggled, crying, "Do something, Turbo Man!" When he got no response, Jamie yelled, "Use your Turbo-Disks!"

Howard looked down at his Turbo Man suit and started patting lights and buttons. "Turbo-Disks? Turbo-Disks?" he muttered. On the gauntlet of his right arm, he found a slot. That looked like where something might shoot out. Howard pushed a button on the gauntlet.

By blind luck alone, Howard's fist was pointed in Myron's direction as dozens of shiny metal disks spit out of the gauntlet and spun through the air. Myron felt the *whap-whap-whap* of impact on his arms, chest, and face. He released Jamie and collapsed in agony. Jamie sprinted across the float to stand behind Howard. The crowd, seeing the bad guy trounced, roared their approval.

With Dementor down, the girls in the booth were able to return to their scripts. "It appears that Turbo Man has saved the day!" crowed Liza.

"But look!" said Gale dramatically. "It's the *Demon Team*—Dementor's evil henchmen!"

A half-dozen hidden doors sprang open on the float and six short Demon Team fighters tumbled out, converging on Howard. Like rowdy little gremlins, they clamped onto Howard's arms and legs and started to pummel him with their little fists and feet.

Jamie jumped clear of the brawl, but before he could figure out how to help Turbo Man, Myron rushed at him. Jamie flexed into karate stance and dropped Myron with a well-placed kick below the belt. He followed through by leaping off the float, leaving Myron on his knees with his eyes bugged wide.

Myron didn't stay down as long as Jamie had hoped—mad desire for the doll had driven the mailman past all pain and reason. Myron lurched back to his feet and charged after the boy.

Jamie jumped up onto the hanging ladder of a fire escape, hoping to climb beyond Myron's reach. But with his longer stride, Myron was at his heels in a second. He scrambled up to the first level of the fire escape. Then he got an idea—he'd make sure nobody could follow by pulling up the ladder behind him. "Get back here, kid!" he shouted once the ladder was up.

Hearing Myron threaten his son gave Howard renewed strength. He shook off the pint-size Demons like a dog shaking off fleas and raced for the edge of the float. A second wave of Demons popped up to block his path. Howard seized the closest one and hefted him overhead. Then with a grunt, Howard threw the Demon into his comrades, knocking them all over the edge and down onto the street. The crowd cheered at Turbo Man's triumph, and one of the Demons muttered, "We'd better be getting overtime for this," before he passed out.

Howard stood on the edge of the float, looking for his son and his foe. The crowd rushed to his aid, pointing toward the fire escape and shouting, "Hurry, Turbo Man! Dementor's getting away! Save the kid! Save him!"

Howard leaped off the float and raced to the fire escape. The first landing was yards above his head, impossible to reach with the ladder drawn up. Howard clenched his fists in frustration as he stared upward. Jamie saw Howard far below and shouted, "Turbo Man! Help!"

Once again, Turbo Man's loyal fans in the crowd had the answer. "Fly, Turbo Man!" they shouted. "Use your jet pack!" Howard looked down at the suit, trying to remember which button did what. He found the most likely one, set his jaw and jabbed it with his thumb. He muttered, "It's Turbo Time!"

To Howard's surprise, flames spewed forth from the jet pack and he found himself rocketing into the air.

Liz elbowed her way through the crowd to the barricade. With one mighty yank, she hurled it aside and ran out into the parade route, her eyes on her son who had made it to the roof of the building. "Jamie!" she cried.

She watched as Myron made it to the roof a moment later. She couldn't hear him shout to Jamie, "Kid, just gimme the doll. You got nowhere else to go!" But she saw her son's reaction. Jamie started climbing up the giant artificial Christmas tree.

Suddenly Liz's view was blocked by a policeman intent on moving her out of the street. "Don't worry, ma'am," he reassured her as he took hold of her arm. "It's all part of the show. Now please step back onto the curb."

"But that's my son up there!" said Liz frantically.

The policeman looked impressed as he looked from Liz to the rooftop. "Oh, he's quite good."

Liz yanked her arm free and yelled at the cop, "He's not part of the show!"

Confusion clouded the officer's face. "He's not?"

"No!" screamed Liz at the top of her lungs.

High above, Howard's stomach did flip-flops as the ground spiraled away beneath his feet. A shrill screaming noise surrounded him, and he was shocked to realize he was its source. As he corkscrewed upward, he slapped at buttons on his chest, looking for a way to stop his mad flight before he disappeared into the sky forever.

He must have pushed something right, because the jet pack's roar ceased and the flame flickered out. Howard felt a moment's relief as his speed lessened and then stopped. And then he dropped like a stone.

Jamie had made it past the heavy bottom branches of the metal Christmas tree. Now he was aiming for the thinner, higher branches. It was his only hope because Dementor followed him whichever way he went, calling out things like, "C'mon, kid. Get back here. You're gonna hurt yourself!" But Jamie was sure that Dementor wasn't worried about a little boy's safety. No, he wanted that doll no matter what. Jamie just hoped the thinner branches above would support a boy but not a big adult. *Something* had to stop Dementor. . . .

Falling to the ground from a great height sharpened Howard's focus amazingly. It only took him two tries to find the ignition button he had originally pressed. He pressed it again. With a lurch, the jet pack reignited, and welcome flames buoyed his body and spirit. By gently playing with the controls, Howard even got an idea of how to steer the rocket. When he managed to fly a straight and level path, he exulted, "I think I've got the hang of this thing!" Then he set his jaw and aimed himself back at Jamie in the giant tree.

Howard could see that Jamie was about two-thirds of the way up the tree. He called out to his son, "I've got you, Jamie!" and stretched his hands out to make a real flying tackle. But shifting his arms changed his flight angle, and Howard missed Jamie by inches, flashing past the tree in the blink of an eye.

Howard cursed under his breath and automatically glanced back, which made his flight path curve again. He kept his eye on his son as he calculated a second pass at the tree, which is why he never saw the banner until he hit it head-on.

The Holiday Wintertainment Parade banner hung from two lampposts and stretched across the parade route. Howard struck near one end of the banner, wrenching it loose from that lamppost. In an instant, the banner wrapped itself around him, and his flight path changed once again, this time from a straight line to a tightening spiral.

The world spun wildly as Howard became a Turbo-powered tetherball, getting wrapped closer and closer to the iron lamppost. With only a few feet of banner to go, the strain became too much for the material and it tore, snapping Howard out of his spiral and back into straight flight again—directly toward an apartment building!

By twisting his body, Howard managed to avoid

hitting the brick wall of the building. Instead, he smashed through a window and rocketed through a nice family apartment.

The family that lived in the apartment was quietly eating at a long dinner table. The father, sitting at the head of the table and totally absorbed in his food, said, "Could you pass the salt?" Suddenly Howard shot through the door at the far end of the room, snatched up the saltshaker at the end of the table, dropped it in front of the father's plate and then zoomed on out the door behind the man—all in under a second. The father, not noticing the red-and-gold blur, picked up the shaker and mumbled, "Thank you."

Howard made it out a window in the apartment without hitting anything and was pleased to find himself back over the parade route again. He glanced back at the building he'd just flown through and breathed a sigh of relief at surviving such a close call. Then he looked forward again, just in time to slam into the brick wall of the building across the street.

Howard and the jet pack had similar reactions—it automatically flamed out and shut down, while he passed out and fell down. The crowd below gasped.

It looked like Jamie was going to run out of tree before Myron ran out of persistence. Jamie was nearly at the top now and the narrow artificial branches wobbled under his weight. Myron was an arm's length or two below him, hugging the central post of the tree because every branch he tried to step on immediately bent when he stepped on it. Myron kept grabbing for Jamie, which made the tree sway back and forth in a stomach-churning rhythm. During one such lunge, two of the guy wires bracing the tree snapped free of their bolts.

The world spun crazily for Jamie as the tree toppled sideways. He shut out everything except holding on until the tree stopped moving. When he opened his eyes again, he found himself hanging far out over the avenue, with only his grip on the tree saving him from a fatal fall.

Not all of the artificial tree's supports had given way. Though bent, the center post of the tree still held even though the tree itself now lay sideways, projecting out over the side of the building. It didn't feel as if it was slipping any farther, but Jamie couldn't count on it for long.

What he could count on, however, was Dementor's mulish persistence. The supervillain hung on to the center post with both hands, his feet dangling in space. But his eyes remained fixed on Jamie, and after a moment, he began to inch closer to the boy, carefully advancing hand over hand. "I'm gonna ask you one more time, kid," he forced out between clenched teeth. "Gimme the toy!"

Jamie had his father's stubbornness. "No way, moron!" he shouted.

Dementor nearly exploded. "It's *Myron!*" he screamed.

Far, far below him, Jamie could see a crumpled Turbo Man slowly dragging himself to his feet. The boy screamed down to his hero, "Turbo Man! Use your Turbo-Rang!"

His son's cries cut through Howard's wooziness. He looked up and snapped to attention when he saw Jamie's predicament. "My what?" he shouted up to the boy.

"The Turbo-Rang!" Jamie called back. "In your holster!"

Howard found the holster attached to his calf. When he pulled out the Turbo-Rang, it snapped open into a graceful curve. Howard hefted it once, getting its feel. Then he leaned far back and threw the Turbo-Rang at Myron with all of his might.

The gleaming arc whizzed upward, fifty feet, a hundred, more. Myron saw it fly straight toward his head. He ducked at the last possible second and laughed as the missile missed him. He turned his attention back to Jamie. Inching closer, Myron finally snatched the special-edition Turbo Man doll from Jamie's backpack. A look of triumph lit up his face.

Wham! The Turbo-Rang performed a tight turn and smashed into the back of Myron's helmet. Stunned, Myron let go of the tree and fell downward. The crowd screamed in horror.

Myron landed in the arms of the giant papier-mâché policeman topping the police department float. The mailman clutched the Turbo Man doll to his chest, crowing, "I got one! I finally got one!"

Dozens of police revolvers clicked around Myron. He looked up to see all the cops who were riding on the float pointing their weapons at him. At the head of the pack stood Officer Hummell. "Release the doll . . . moron," Hummell ordered.

Defeated, Myron dropped the doll into Hummell's outstretched hand. Then he raised his hands slowly over his head and disappeared as a wall of uniforms closed in on him.

High above, Jamie was completely unaware of Myron's fate. All the boy's attention was fixed on his tiring fingers which were losing their grip on the Christmas tree. He couldn't feel anything in his arms anymore. He risked a look below him and saw Myron on the police float. But the float had moved on, and there was nothing but hard street below him now.

Then he fell.

11

Howard heard Liz scream as she saw her son plummet earthward. He slapped the ignition button on his chest and roared into the air on a column of fire. Howard finally had a feeling for how to steer the jet pack and he raced against gravity to reach his son in time.

Jamie was only a few feet from the ground when he felt the strong arms of Turbo Man grab him and bear him up and away from the onrushing ground. Together they swooped in a graceful curve up and then back down toward the parade. Jamie beamed at his hero. "Thanks, Turbo Man. I knew you'd save me."

Howard looked at his son in his arms and his heart nearly burst with pride. "Glad you could count on me," he said as he settled gently to the ground.

The crowd had been cheering wildly since the daring

midair rescue, but now they redoubled their shouts as Howard landed in front of Liz and Johnny. "Awesome" was all Johnny could say.

Striking his best superhero pose, Howard offered Jamie to Liz. "Here you go, ma'am," he said in his filtered voice.

Before Liz could do more than smile, Jamie burst out with, "Mom! Did you *see* that? I was flying with *Turbo Man!* He saved me from *Dementor!* It was the *coolest!* Did you see? *Did* you?"

Liz hugged Jamie tightly. "I saw. I saw," she said. There were tears in her eyes as she looked up at the costumed man. "Thank you, sir," she said, choked with emotion. "Whoever you are. Thank you so much. I don't think you know how important he is to me."

Howard smiled gravely. "I think I've got an idea," he said softly.

Liz looked down at Jamie and saw a look of sadness cross the boy's face. "Jamie?" she said. "What's the matter?"

Jamie seemed to shrink. "It's just . . ." he began hesitantly. "I wish Dad coulda been here. You know. To see me fly and all. He woulda loved that." Jamie's eyes brimmed with sadness. "But he didn't come. And it's all my fault. He's mad at me. We had a fight on the phone and I kinda yelled at him. . . ." His voice faltered.

"Oh, honey, it's not your fault, really . . ." began Liz.

Howard squatted so he could be face-to-face with Jamie. "Your dad's not mad at you, Jamie. I know that. For a *fact.*" He tapped Jamie on the chest. "Why, your dad loves you more than anything in the whole wide world. You're his all-time favorite person . . ."

"Really?" asked Jamie, blinking back tears.

"The problem was, he just didn't realize what was *really* important—until it was almost too late."

Jamie looked hard at the Turbo Man faceplate. "How do you know all that?"

Howard flipped up the visor. "Who would know better than me?"

"Dad?!"

"Howard?!"

Howard grinned at his son and his wife. "Right here," he said, gathering Jamie in for a hug. He stood up, lifting Jamie with him, and beamed at Liz. "You two are more important to me than anything. I'm sorry if it seems like I've forgotten that lately. I love you both."

Liz enfolded her son and her husband in her arms and kissed Howard warmly. They pressed together until Officer Hummell walked up behind them, holding out the special-edition Turbo Man doll. "I think this belongs to you, young man," he said to Jamie. He addressed Howard's back. "And as for you, Turbo Man, well, we could use a man like you on the force—"

Howard turned around to shake Hummell's outstretched hand. "Thanks. I'll keep that in mind," he said. Officer Hummell said nothing. He just stood, stunned, as Howard and his family moved away.

Jamie led them over to where Myron Larrabee, surrounded by cops, stared at his hands and sobbed. "I *had* it. It was right in my hands . . ."

Jamie looked from the doll in his hands to his father. Then he walked up to Myron and held out the doll to him. "Here," the boy said to the mailman. "Merry Christmas."

Myron clutched the doll to his chest, tearful and ecstatic at the same time. "Thank you! Thank you!" he babbled. "Sorry 'bout almost dropping you off that building. . . ."

Liz and Howard joined Jamie. "But I thought you wanted that doll more than anything," Liz said to her son.

Jamie shrugged. "What do I need the *doll* for?" He pointed at Howard. "I've got the *real* Turbo Man at home!"

They hugged again, but this time, only for a second. Half the town suddenly crowded around them, cheering for the rescue, cheering for the grand show and cheering just for the fun of it. Howard was hoisted up on many shoulders and carried back to the Turbo Man float to shouts from the throng: "Turbo Man! He saved the parade! He's a hero!"

Ahead of them strutted Jamie, proclaiming to one and all, "That's my dad! That's my dad!"

Behind them, almost unnoticed, Myron was led away by the cops. He pleaded with them, "Okay, fellas, you got me. I give up." He held the special doll up. "But just lemme make this one final delivery. Please?"

12

The Langston family sat before a roaring fire in their living room late on Christmas Eve. Howard and Liz snuggled together on the sofa while Jamie sat at his father's feet, looking up worshipfully and continuing to ask questions. "Dad, where does Booster sleep when you come home at night?"

Liz smiled fondly at Howard, who still couldn't seem to get his side of the story across to his son. "Look, Jamie—I'm not really Turbo Man. Let me explain again. See, I was coming to the parade—"

Jamie was up and in karate combat pose. His foot lashed out at an imaginary foe. "Show me again how you kicked Dementor's butt!"

Howard looked helplessly at Liz. She smiled wryly at her husband's predicament, then impishly took Jamie's side. "Come on!" she urged. "One more time!"

It took Howard only a second to fold. "All right. So there I was, standing on the front of my float, waving to my fans . . ." He pantomimed the action. "When suddenly I see *Dementor* swinging over the crowd—"

The doorbell rang, interrupting Howard's reenactment. He got up to answer it, winking to Jamie. "Maybe that's Booster."

It wasn't a six-foot-tall pink saber-toothed tiger, it was Ted Maltin and his son Johnny at the door. Ted looked uncomfortable. "Uh, hi, Howard."

"Hey, Ted," Howard answered. "Care for some *eggnog?"* He smirked.

Ted gingerly touched the large bruise on his forehead. "Uh . . . no thanks," he mumbled.

Johnny tugged at Ted's sleeve. "Dad . . ." Johnny stage-whispered. "You *promised!"*

Ted's face grew a plastic smile. "Oh. Oh—right. Um . . . *Turbo Man . . ."* Ted stumbled over the name slightly. "Johnny wanted to know if he could come in and play with you for a while."

Howard beamed an honest smile at Ted's discomfort. "Why, I think that'd be all right," he said expansively.

"Excellent!" shouted Johnny, and raced inside to find Jamie, passing Liz along the way. She came and stood at the door next to her husband. "Hello, Ted," she said frostily.

Ted continued to stand at the door, hemming and hawing. Finally, without looking Howard or Liz in the eye, he stammered, "Look, I just came by . . . to apologize to both of you. It's a very emotional time of year, and I think perhaps earlier I may have gotten caught up in some emotions that weren't quite . . . *appropriate.* And I hope my behavior hasn't affected what up until now has been a warm and mutually respectful relationship." Ted squirmed visibly. "You've always been so kind to me." His voice broke. "I'm so ashamed," he said, sobbing.

"Oh, Ted, please," said Liz dryly. She turned and walked back into the living room, leaving Howard to loom over their humiliated neighbor.

Ted pulled himself together and pleaded with Howard. "If there's *any* way I could make that up to you—" he began.

Howard smirked. "Actually," he drawled, "my driveway *could* use a little shoveling. I've been meaning to get to it, but . . ."

Ted brightened. "I'll get on it right away! Anything else?"

"We need firewood."

"I'm on top of it."

"Oh, and we're out of milk."

"I know where there's a convenience store open." Ted backed away.

Howard couldn't resist. "And how about some fresh-squeezed orange juice?"

Ted saluted as he moved back. "No problem, Howard." Ted caught himself being too flip. "I mean . . .

Turbo Man," he corrected respectfully. He turned and raced for his car.

Howard's happiness was complete as he returned to his place next to Liz on the sofa. Jamie was swooping around Johnny, showing him what it was like to fly. Liz snuggled closer to Howard and kissed him gently on the cheek. "I can't remember a better Christmas," she murmured.

"I couldn't agree more," said Howard, drawing her close. Jamie "flew" by again. Howard looked at him lovingly. "You know, from now on I'm going to spend a little less time with my mattresses and a lot more time with my family. When it comes to you and Jamie, if I snooze—*I* lose."

Liz kissed him warmly and then settled into the curve of his arm. "You know, Howard, I've been thinking, too," she began. "Everything you went through today for Jamie . . . well, it really shows how much you love him."

Howard nodded, basking in the praise.

"And if you're willing to do all of that for him—just for a present," she continued. "Well, it sort of makes me wonder . . ."

"What?" said Howard, eyes closed, at peace with the world.

Liz looked up at him coyly. "What did you get me?"

Howard's eyes snapped wide open, panicked.

About the Authors

Stolen from Gypsies as a child, David Cody Weiss was raised in suburban comfort until his teens. Then his true heritage claimed him, and he broke loose of the middle-class straitjacket, going forth and having many jobs (no two alike!). When he acquired a wife and a partner, he decided that becoming a writer was better than working for a living. His goal is to become independently wealthy, and he thanks you for buying this book.

Delivered one Christmas morning by reindeer instead of a stork, Bobbi JG Weiss has spent most of her life avoiding Reality and to this day still keeps up a personal correspondence with Rudolph. Clinging to the belief that cartoons are real, that cats speak English, and that coffee bestows superpowers, she is fit for no other profession than that of writer. With her husband she has penned novels, comic books, animation, trading cards, CD-ROMs, and dumb little comic strips for orange juice cartons. One day she hopes to become a cartoon.